THE HELLSFIRE LAWMAN

For seven scorching days and bitter nights Sam Kyler had dogged the three outlaws like a silent, deadly shadow. And now the chase was about to end. Shotgun Sam rode into Jericho, his sawed-off, double-barreled shotgun hanging from his saddle, and Kyler knew he would once again be forced to use it against the desperadoes who had robbed him and slung mud on his name.

RAY HOGAN

THE HELLSFIRE LAWMAN

Complete and Unabridged

LINFORD
Leicester

First Linford Edition
published May 1989

British Library CIP Data

Hogan, Ray, *1908–*
The hellsfire lawman.—Large print ed.—
Linford western library
I. Title
813′.54[F]

ISBN 0-7089-6711-6

Published by
F. A. Thorpe (Publishing) Ltd.
Anstey, Leicestershire
Set by Rowland Phototypesetting Ltd.
Bury St. Edmunds, Suffolk
Printed and bound in Great Britain by
T. J. Press (Padstow) Ltd., Padstow, Cornwall

1

FOR seven scorching days and bitter nights he had been on their trail—a haunched, persistent shape on a bay horse dogging the three outlaws like a silent, deadly shadow. And now the chase was about to end.

In the beginning they had known of his presence and that fact, he finally realized, was defeating him. As long as he pursued they would continue to run and never permit him to draw within striking distance. And so Sam Kyler had come to a decision; he had chosen a time and place when he was clearly visible to them and turned back.

He took no chance on the ruse failing. They would make certain he had given up before relaxing their vigilance, and to convince them, he wasted ten miles of riding, cutting east through the rabbitbrush choked arroyos and across the snakeweed covered hills before he began to circle.

The scheme had worked. The outlaws were

1

just below him now, moving leisurely, no more than a quarter mile distant. It would be easy to close in and capture them—or have it out with guns if they so chose. And then the long, tedious hunt would be at an end.

Kyler's mouth hardened as he looked down upon the men. . . . Joe Grimsby, thick shoulders slumped, was apparently asleep in the saddle. . . . Shad Collins rode with one leg hooked over the horn as he sought to relieve his tired muscles. . . . Ed Tilton was rolling himself a quirley, his elbows extended as he worked with paper and tobacco.

Once they had been his friends—now all were deadly enemies, men he must face and possibly kill, or else be killed in the confrontation. The change had come abruptly, a little more than a week ago when they had all been working for Arch Clayborn on his A-Bar-C spread in Texas.

The four of them had been fairly close companions both on the job and off, and when Clayborn had turned over to Kyler a wallet containing a thousand dollars in cash with which to pay for a small herd of cattle he had purchased from a New Mexico rancher. Sam had naturally chosen his three friends to assist him in driving back the stock.

On his own since the age of fifteen, knocking about from job to job, town to town, Sam Kyler had come to know the way of the world only too well; he was aware that a desire for money could do strange and terrible things to a man's mind and character, but he never expected to have the fact driven home to him so forcibly— and by those he considered trustworthy.

It occurred on the second night out as they lay in their blankets around a dying fire. He had awakened to an unnatural sound, opened his eyes to glimpse Grimsby standing over him, arm upraised. He had tried to dodge the blow but the inner warning had come too late. The outlaw's gun butt had smashed into his skull with a sickening force.

Near daylight Kyler had regained consciousness and struggled to his feet. Clayborn's thousand dollars was gone—and with it Grimsby, Tilton and Shad Collins. It was noon, however, before he had fully collected his scattered senses and located the tracks of the departed horses. Immediately he had begun the pursuit.

There had been no doubt in Sam Kyler's mind that he would eventually overtake the outlaws; he was that sort of individual—patient, determined and inflexible once he had committed himself. What did concern him then was what Arch Clayborn would conclude when he discovered his foreman had dropped out of sight with the money entrusted to his care.

Clayborn had been a good man to work for, and Sam at first had intended to pause long enough in some town and send a letter to the rancher giving him full particulars as to what had happened. But as the days wore on and the trail of the outlaws led steadily north, missing all settlements of any size where he could have dispatched a note, the advisability of not getting in touch with Clayborn became more apparent.

By then, he knew, the rancher would have made up his mind, and closed it. No explanation would suffice. The only thing that would satisfy him would be the return of his money.

Thus Sam Kyler had chosen that course; he would recover the one thousand dollars stolen from him and return it to Clayborn. It would be the only means by which he could convince the rancher of his innocence. Besides, writing Clayborn could prove dangerous; likely his first move, upon learning the whereabouts of his missing foreman, would be to notify the law.

And Kyler did not want that. Because of his own misplaced trust he had lost Clayborn's money; by his own efforts he would recover it. Locked in a cell somewhere he would be powerless to accomplish such.

He reached down, rubbed at the bay's sweat-soaked neck, his eyes never straying from the outlaws. He had no liking for the chore that lay ahead but he knew there was no avoiding it.

During the last year of the war, while serving under the command of bearded Bill Hardee in the Carolina campaign, he had witnessed enough bloodshed to last him for an entire lifetime. But even there it had not ended. When the war was over he had become a shotgun guard in the gold rich country of Nevada; later he had served a time as a deputy marshal, following that with a stint at ramrodding trail herds from Texas to the Kansas markets.

When he had signed up with Arch Clayborn as foreman he had figured the heavy forty-five in his holster and the sawed-off, ten gauge shotgun hanging from his saddle, with which he was so proficient, could be put away for good insofar as his fellow man was concerned. Now he was again faced with using them.

That thought brought a stillness to his

features, but after a moment he shrugged off the melancholy mood and brushed at the sweat beading his forehead. There are times when a man must accept and discharge a disagreeable duty.

Pushing his hat to the back of his head, he drew his sixgun, thumbed open the loading gate and checked the cylinder. It was ready. Leaning forward, he pulled the shotgun from its boots, made certain of its charge. Satisfied with both weapons, he touched the bay with his spurs lightly and moved out from behind the clump of cedar where he had halted.

Immediately he hauled back on the reins. A sound had reached him. A cry for help, he thought. Frowning, he sat motionless in the saddle, listening into the heat filled hush. Somewhere below a jay scolded noisily. A ground squirrel chattered an angry reply. And then the cry came again.

"Help! . . . If they's somebody up there on the trail—how about givin' me a hand?"

"Nope . . . Nothin' bad I reckon. Got skinned up a mite and sort of twisted my leg . . . Expect I'll live." He extended a weathered hand. "Folks what knows me calls me Wasco."

"Glad to know you, Wasco. I'm Sam Kyler. How long you been hanging to that rock?"

"Since daylight. Sure was gettin' right uncomfortable."

Kyler finished coiling his rope, got to his feet. He looked again to the north, came back to Wasco. "What happened?"

Wasco swore, wagged his grizzled head. His iron gray hair was long, hung about his face, made it appear even sharper.

"Danged bobcat spooked old Buck . . . Went shyin' too close to the edge. Next thing I knew I was hangin' onto that there ledge and Buck was kickin' his last in all them rocks below me."

The old puncher sat up, brushed at the dirt plastered to the front of his linsey-woolsy shirt. "Reckon you're a stranger in these parts. Don't recollect ever layin' eyes on you afore."

"Guess I am," Kyler replied, turning to hang his rope on the bay.

Wasco frowned, then grinned. "Ain't

9

meanin' to be nosy, Sam. Just talkin'. Ain't every day a man gets his neck saved."

"Forget it," Kyler said in the same clipped way. "You live around here close?"

"Nope. Just ridin' through. Ain't got no real home—unless you figure now and then when I get myself a job somewheres."

Sam Kyler continued to work with his rope, securing it to the saddle. Wasco couldn't be left to fend for himself. Without a horse, and having an injured leg, he wouldn't last long. Unconsciously, he glanced once more in the direction taken by the outlaws. If he delayed to help Wasco he would lose them sure.

"Was three, four riders by here earlier this mornin'," Wasco said. "Done a lot of hollerin' but seems they didn't hear me." He paused, his wise old eyes pulled down into slits as he studied Kyler. "They got somethin' to do with your bein' here? You maybe chasin' them?"

Kyler shrugged, said, "Think you can ride?"

The old puncher chuckled. "Reckon I had that comin'. Always stickin' my nose in other people's business. Wouldn't surprise me none was you to knock it slanchwise just to be teachin' me a lesson."

"I'm trailing them," Kyler said. "And I'm losing them—fast. How about it?"

Wasco bobbed his head, pulled himself. upright. "Leg's a mite stiff," he said, taking a few experimental steps, "But I reckon I can make out, seein' as how you're in a hurry."

"Don't aim for you to walk. Asked if you could ride. The bay can carry us both."

"Sure would slow you down a powerful lot. Better just go on."

"Not that short of time. There a town anywhere near here?"

"Sure. Place called Jericho. Real stemwinder of a town. But it ain't so close. Reckon it'd be dark, time we could make it."

Kyler considered thoughtfully. "Which way?"

"North. Way you was headed. And them others?"

Sam Kyler relaxed slightly. That was welcome news. The outlaws, on the move for over a week, and now believing themselves free of him, would undoubtedly halt in the first town they reached. Perhaps his stopping to aid Wasco wouldn't prove so costly after all.

A moment later Wasco corroborated his

thoughts, and then added: "Say, you ain't no lawman, are you?"

"No . . . Why?"

"Jericho ain't exactly no healthy spot for a badge toter. Lot of the wild bunch hangs out there."

That would suit Joe Grimsby and the others. They would feel right at home with their kind —and believe themselves to be safe. Sam nodded at Wasco.

"Let's move out . . ."

The old puncher flung a glance toward the bluff, clawed at the whiskers on his chin. "Well, if you ain't mindin' too much, everythin' I own in this here world's down there on Buck. Sort of like to collect it first."

Kyler said, "Sure," and began to shake loose his rope for the second time. Securing one end to a stout juniper, he tested it briefly, then walked to the rim of the butte.

"You want the whole works?"

"Sure would be obliged."

Bracing himself against the taut rope, Sam went over the edge and lowered himself to where the horse lay. He was in for another half hour's delay, he realized, but if the outlaws stopped in Jericho it wouldn't matter. If for some reason they did not—well, he'd just have to start all over again.

Stripping the dead animal of its gear did not take long. Fastening it to the end of the lariat, Kyler waited for Wasco to draw it up and return the rope to him.

When that was done the old puncher said, "You want I should tie onto the bay, let him do the work?"

"Let him rest . . . I can make it," Sam answered.

He climbed out of the deep wash, going up hand over hand, digging the pointed toes of his boots into the steep side of the bluff to assist him in the ascent. When he reached level ground, breathing heavily, he paused, stared curiously at Wasco. The rider was strapping on an ancient pistol that evidently had been inside his saddlebags.

"You figure on having to use that iron when we get to Jericho?"

"If it's needful," Wasco said. "I ain't no greenhorn when it comes to handlin' a gun. Just never seen no use of packin' it around 'less'n there was a reason."

"And now you do . . ."

Wasco hawked, spat. "With what I figure you

got in mind to do, you'll be needin' somebody watchin' your backside."

Kyler shook his head. "No need for you to mix in my trouble . . ."

"Maybe . . . But seems I already have. Wasn't for me you'd done slipped up on them sidewinders and had them hog-tied for market. Now the job's goin' to be a heap harder. Only right I return the favor . . ."

The belt and holster in place, Wasco made a few testing passes at drawing his old cedar handled weapon. That he was no stranger to the sixgun was apparent. Kyler smiled at him.

"Be pleased to have you siding me," he said. "Now, climb aboard and I'll hand you up your gear."

Wasco crossed to the bay, crawled stiffly to a seat behind the cantle of Kyler's saddle. Sleeving the sweat from his jaws, he looked down at Sam.

"I'm all set . . ."

Kyler hoisted the old rider's belonging to the back of the bay, resting it partly on the man's shoulders and partly on the hindquarters of the horse, and then swung to the saddle. The bay bunched slightly at the load but he made no move to balk.

14

"You figure he can make it?" Wasco asked as they turned down-slope.

Sam nodded. "Be slow going, but he can do it."

3

THE bay made better time than expected. It was shortly before five o'clock when they broke suddenly from a cluster of round topped hills and saw Jericho before them.

Kyler pulled up at the end of the street. The settlement was considerably larger than he had expected and he made this observation to Wasco.

"Got a reason to be," the old puncher said. "Only town in this part of the Strip."

"Strip?"

"Yeh . . . We're in the panhandle west of the Indian Territory. Maybe you've heard it called No-Man's-Land . . . Lots of folks call it that 'cause it ain't claimed by nobody. . . ."

Sam nodded. "See now why the outlaws like it."

He allowed his gaze to probe the town slowly. The single street was narrow and dusty. He could see a hotel, the Fargo; it was a ramshackle, sun-grayed building with a high false front. Beyond it was a general store, a livery barn and corral; an office where a doctor and a barber plied their professions.

Elsewhere there was a feed store, a cafe, gun and harness shop, several saloons—the largest of which offered gambling and dancing as well as liquor. A white steepled church, badly in need of paint, stood at the far end of the town, and beyond it lay a scatter of residences.

There were no pedestrians in sight, but in front of the Fargo he saw a buggy and a half dozen horses drawn up to the rail. His glance drifted on, came to an abrupt halt when his eyes settled upon three more horses tethered at the side of the Palace, the largest saloon.

Kyler's mouth hardened. The mounts were those of Grimsby, Tilton and Shad Collins. Luck was with him. They had done as expected.

"Any sign of them jaspers you're huntin'?" Wasco asked.

Kyler said, "Horses there at the Palace . . . The ones they were ridin'."

"Figured they'd hole up here. . . . What's next?"

"Little talk with them," Kyler said, and put the bay in motion.

They moved on down the street. As they

drew abreast the Fargo Sam was conscious of several men filing out onto the porch, lining up to watch him pass. He gave them a brief glance. Cattlemen and several merchants, he guessed. Having some sort of a meeting.

He headed directly for the Palace, wasting no moments on preliminaries. The cafe, he noted as the bay walked through the ankle deep dust, was called Mrs. Ashwick's. The doctor's name was Patton—Carl Patton. The general store bore the sign SOL WEIL in faded lettering across its front. A Fred Turnbull operated the harness shop.

Swinging his horse up to the Palace's hitchrack, he sat quiet while Wasco let his gear fall to the ground and dropped beside it. Only then did Kyler leave the saddle. He stood there for a moment, his face still and hard cornered as he looked off toward the flats and then, seemingly almost regretfully, he came back to the business at hand.

Reaching down, he touched the handle of the pistol at his hip as though assuring himself of its presence. Then, half turning, he drew the short barreled shotgun from its scabbard, slung it into the crook of his left arm. He paused, glanced at Wasco.

18

"Still no reason you should mix in this."

"Got a dang good reason, far as I'm concerned," the old puncher replied.

Sam Kyler shrugged, said, "All right . . . But it's my fight."

"Sure . . . Sure . . . Won't go hornin' in unless you need me."

Kyler nodded, moved up the steps to the gallery of the Palace and walked slowly toward the batwing doors.

He paused there, Wasco a stride behind him. Inside he could hear the drone of conversation, the laughter of women. A man swore in a deep voice and a chair scraped across a bare floor. Again he touched the pistol at his hip, and then moved forward, pushed into the smoke-filled room.

He rocked slightly to one side as he collided with a puncher on his way out. The man staggered, off balance, face going taut with anger.

"Watch where you're goin'—dammit!"

Kyler, never removing his eyes from the patrons ranged along the bar, nodded briefly, said, "Sorry."

"Sorry—nothin'!" the puncher growled and reached for Sam's arm. "I ain't takin'—"

"Keep movin', son," Wasco cut in quietly,

19

blocking the rider's way. "Sure ain't the right time to be startin' a ruckus with him."

Kyler walked deeper into the room, taking slow, easy steps, paying no more attention to the offended rider. He came to a halt a third of the distance to the bar. Abruptly his drifting glance settled on three men seated at a corner table.

The murmur of voices died gradually. In the hush Sam saw Collins and his two companions lift their heads lazily, look questioningly toward the crowd. When they saw him they stiffened with surprise.

Men crowded through the batwings behind Kyler. He heard the thud of their boot-heels, flipped his gaze to the back-bar mirror, as quickly returned it to the outlaws. A group of townsmen and ranchers coming in for a drink. The ones he had noticed on the porch of the Fargo. . . . He dismissed them from his mind.

Moving deliberately, watchfully, Kyler headed for the outlaws. A dozen paces short he stopped. From the tail of his eye he saw Wasco saunter up to the bar, take a position against it. He placed his direct glance on Grimsby, Ed Tilton and the younger Collins. In the deep hush his low voice reached every corner of the room.

"I'll take the money. . . ."

Joe Grimsby forced a smile. His teeth showed whitely through the dark stubble of his beard. He nodded to Collins.

"Told you we should've done the job up right. Now we got to do it all over again."

There was a forced quality to his voice that betrayed the confidence he was attempting to display. Shad Collins made no reply. Tilton shifted nervously, careful to keep his hands in sight on the table. Out in the street a dog barked, and at Calderone's stable, an anvil rang musically as a blacksmith worked at his trade.

"Stand up!"

Kyler's tone was sharp, carried the promise of violence. Collins rose at once, overturning his chair in his haste. Tilton followed. Joe Grimsby did not move. Kyler studied the man coldly for a long ten seconds, then shifted the wicked looking shotgun to his right hand. Lazily, Grimsby pulled himself upright.

"The money," Sam repeated. "Take off the belt. Lay it on the table."

Tilton flung a worried glance at Grimsby. His

eyes were abnormally bright and sweat glistened on his skin. "For chrissake—give it to him!"

The fixed smile hung on Grimsby's lips. He shook his head. "What's eatin' you jaspers? Three of us—only one of him."

"Odds don't mean nothin' to him," Shad Collins said.

Grimsby's eyes flickered with a cunning light. He shrugged. "Reckon any man's real big holdin' a crowd killer."

Sam Kyler considered the outlaw for a time. He shifted the shotgun back to his left hand, carefully laid it on a near table. Someone at the bar moved, knocked a glass to the floor. At the shattering sound the outlaws jumped. Kyler seemed not to hear.

"He ain't nothin' but a man—same as me," Grimsby muttered as though trying to convince himself.

"You taking off that money belt?" Kyler pressed quietly.

Joe Grimsby shook his head. "You want it— you take it."

Kyler's hand swept down, came up swiftly with his forty-five at full cock. "You're calling the play," he said, moving forward slowly. "If you don't figure to die suddenly, stand easy."

22

Reaching out with his left hand, he ripped Grimsby's shirt front open. The dull glint of a buckle told him he had guessed right. The older man was carrying the money belt.

Sam flicked Tilton and the sullen faced Collins with a calculating glance, and then released the tongue of the buckle. The belt came free. He stepped back, yanked the leather pocketed strap from the outlaw's waist.

Grimsby yelled. He lunged to one side, clawed for his pistol. In the same instant Ed Tilton threw himself to the opposite direction, went for his gun.

Kyler fired as Grimsby went to his knees triggering his weapon. Sam loosed one bullet at the outlaw, wheeled to Tilton. Both guns blasted— almost as one. Glass tinkled as Tilton's bullet smashed into a shelf behind the bar, destroyed a pyramid of beer mugs.

Kyler, never breaking his smooth spin, faced Collins. The young outlaw stood with his hands raised above his head.

"Not me!" he yelled frantically.

Sam Kyler's half bent shape relaxed slightly. A hard grin pulled at his lips. "Maybe you'd like me to turn my back."

23

Collins shook his head. "Wasn't none of my idea—taking the money . . ."

"Seems you went along with it all the same."

"Nothing I could do."

Kyler raked the outlaw with his cold glance. "You had a choice. . . . You could've sided with me. Now, step out here—and keep your hands up high."

Collins moved from behind the table, circling Tilton's lifeless body. A sigh ran through the saloon as tension eased. Kyler motioned to Wasco.

"Take his gun."

The old puncher limped to Shad Collin's side, pulled the man's weapon from its holster and shoved it under his belt.

"Go get the law."

Wasco started to turn. The bartender said, "We ain't got no lawman, mister. Buried the last one about a month ago."

Kyler frowned. He glanced at the bartender, tossed the money belt to him.

"Name's Sam Kyler," he said. "These three men jumped me back in Texas, robbed me of that belt. Open it. Ought to find a thousand dollars and a letter from a man named Clayborn introducing me to another man called Blye. . . .

24

Was on my way to buy some stock for Clayborn when it happened."

The bartender laid the belt on the counter and opened its pockets. He removed the folds of currency and began to thumb through the bills. Finally he looked up.

"Letter's here—but there ain't no thousand dollars. I make it about nine hundred."

Kyler's jaw hardened. He stared at Collins. The outlaw shifted nervously.

"Grimsby must've got it. He was paying for everything."

Sam pointed at the dead man. "Drag him over here."

Collins turned obediently, and taking his one-time partner by the arm, pulled him into the open.

"Dig into his pockets. I want what's left of the money he took."

Collins hesitated momentarily, then dropped to his knees and began to rifle Grimsby's clothing. He located some loose change and a small roll of bills.

"Count it."

Shad sorted through the currency, ticked off the silver. "Twenty dollars, thereabouts."

Kyler nodded. He would have to make up

the loss himself. "Give it to the bartender," he directed.

Collins crossed to the counter, laid the money before the aproned man who added it to that in the pouches. That done, Kyler picked up the belt, hung it over his shoulder.

"There a bank in this town?"

"Nope. Dalhart—that's the closest."

"Had one once," someone volunteered, "but the outlaws busted it—raidin' it all the time."

Kyler accepted the information with no change of expression. He placed his attention on Collins. "Don't aim to be bothered with you," he said. "Get on your horse and start riding—and don't come back. We ever cross trails again it'll be a different story."

Shad Collins stirred sullenly. He glanced at his gun tucked under Wasco's belt. "My iron?"

"Won't need it," Kyler said coldly. "Move out." He shifted his eyes to Wasco. "See that he does."

The outlaw, trailed by the old puncher, started immediately for the door. Kyler picked up his shotgun, turned to watch Collins leave. At once an excited buzz of voices broke out.

A tall, graying man dressed in the everyday work clothes of a rancher detached himself from a group standing at the far end of the bar and began to work his way through the crowd. He was one of those who came in last, Sam recalled. He glanced inquiringly at the older man who halted before him.

"Something on your mind?"

The rancher smiled. "Sure is, Mr. Kyler. Name's Tolliver . . . We'd like to talk to you."

4

KYLER settled slowly on his heels. Being confronted by irate citizens indignant over some incident such as had just transpired there in the Palace was not new to him. Tolliver, however, was smiling.

"What about?"

"A job," the rancher replied.

Out in the street there was the quick drum of a horse pulling away fast. A moment later Wasco pushed through the batwings, came back into the room.

"Took off like the heel flies was after him," he said, grinning.

Sam nodded, looked again to Tolliver. "Who said I was hunting a job?"

"Nobody. Just figured you might be interested . . ."

"We ever met before?"

Tolliver shook his head. "Recognized you when you rode in. Saw you down in Texas once, but you don't know me. We're willing to pay plenty for the kind of help you could give us."

28

"We?"

Tolliver waved carelessly toward the group of men still standing at the end of the bar. "Cattlemen's Association. Some of the merchants."

Kyler considered. Curious, he asked: "How much is plenty?"

"Well—we haven't had time to get together, and come up with a figure, but I'd say several hundred dollars. . . . Be about a week's work."

That kind of money could only mean squatter trouble, or rustlers; possibly a range war. Kyler shrugged.

"Guess it's my gun you're figuring to hire."

Tolliver smiled frankly. "Guess you could say that. Before you make up your mind to say no, why not let us talk it over with you?"

"No harm in listening."

"Right . . . Just give me about thirty minutes to get the men together. We've been holding a meeting over in the Fargo Hotel. I'll call them back, see you there."

Sam said, "Fine. Gives us a chance to get a bite to eat." He paused, pointed at Wasco, added, "That offer include my partner?"

"Sure does," Tolliver said, and wheeling, rejoined his friends.

Wasco moved in closer. "Now, what's that all about?"

"Tell you later," Kyler answered and crossed to the bar. Reaching into his pocket he produced a double eagle, laid it on the counter. Parting with it would leave him almost broke but he felt the obligation was his.

"This ought to cover the burying," he said to the bartender. "If it won't, let me know."

"Be enough," the man said. "I'll see to it."

"And there's two horses out at the side of the building. Wasco, here, wants the black. Somebody else can have the other one. . . . Maybe you know a family who could use him."

The bartender's face brightened. "Bet I do, Mr. Kyler. Folks by the name of Lindsay. Mare of theirs up and died with the colic the other day. They sure do need a horse."

"Obliged to you if you'll see they get him."

"Can have the gear off'n the black, too," Wasco said.

The bartender smiled again. "They'll be mighty grateful to you both. And I expect they'll be wantin' to thank you personal. You be around?"

"Doubt it," Kyler said. "You just see they get him. That's all the thanks we need."

Turning to Wasco, he said, "Let's get something to eat," and headed for the doorway.

They stepped out onto the porch, immediately drawing the attention of a dozen or so persons scattered along the board sidewalk. Ignoring their curious glances, they waded through the dust of the street and entered the restaurant. The place was empty and they had their choice of a half dozen tables. Selecting one near the window that afforded them a good view of the town, they sat down.

Mrs. Ashwick proved to be a young woman somewhere in her late twenties. Attractive and neat, she came from the rear of the building and advanced in quick, brisk steps and halted before them. She had brown eyes, Sam noted, and when she spoke her voice was low and firm.

"I expect the town has already thanked you for what you've done . . . Let me add mine."

Kyler looked at her in surprise. "Thanked me? For what?"

"Ridding us of those outlaws . . . Men like that pretty well have their own way around here now."

Kyler shifted on his chair. "Was a personal matter, ma'am. Had nothing to do with your town."

31

"Nevertheless, it was a big favor. Have you been approached yet about the job?"

Sam stared at her. Things certainly got around fast. He nodded. "We're meeting with Tolliver and the others in a half hour . . ."

Mrs. Ashwick bit at her lips angrily. "Might have known the ranchers would step in first!"

Kyler shook his head helplessly. "Don't rightly know what you're talking about."

"The marshal's job. We need a good man to fill the vacancy left when our last lawman was killed . . . Not that he was much good. Outlaws ran wild—sometimes actually took over the town. Not safe around here for anyone anymore."

"Sounds like you sure do need a lawman," Wasco drawled. "Maybe three or four."

"One would be enough—if he had the courage to stand up to the outlaws," Mrs. Ashwick said. "That's why I hoped the men had spoken . . . to . . ." Her voice trailed off into silence.

"Maybe they intend to," Kyler said, more to relieve the awkward moment than anything else.

"Too late now. If Tom Tolliver and the ranchers have already talked to you—"

"All it amounts to so far—talk. And we haven't done much of that. Like I said, we're meeting them later."

"You'll go to work for them," she said wearily. "The ranchers always get their way."

Sam Kyler shrugged. He didn't know what it was all about but it seemed everyone was taking a lot for granted.

"Could be," he said. "But there's a little matter everybody's overlooking. I'm not wanting a job. I've got one—back in Texas. Leastwise, I figure I have once I get things cleared up."

Mrs. Ashwick sighed, straightened the front of her white apron. "What would you like to eat?"

"Steak and potatoes," Kyler said promptly. "Plenty of coffee. And some pie." He glanced at Wasco. "Suit you?"

"Right down to a frog's hair . . . Been doin' my own cookin' for so long I don't hardly know what a good meal looks like."

Mrs. Ashwick turned away, returned immediately with mugs of coffee and a plate of warm biscuits and butter. "This will tide you over until I get the meat fried," she said and again retired.

Wasco took a deep swallow of coffee and reached for a biscuit. "What you reckon this here job is Tolliver was yappin' about?"

"Hard to say. Seems to be worth plenty to him—and the others."

"You goin' to be interested?"

Kyler studied his cup. "Don't know. Figure I can go back to work for Clayborn after I explain what happened. But I'm not sure I want to. Felt good traveling again."

"Gets a powerful hold on a man, all right. Ain't ever been able to shuck it, myself."

"Tolliver said it would take about a week. If the job and the pay's right, you willing to sign on?"

"Ain't agin' it. Lot depends on what you do."

Kyler glanced at the old puncher and smiled. It was good having him around. He nodded. "Soon as we eat we'll go see what it's all about."

5

SAM KYLER and Wasco halted as they
entered the Fargo and turned left into a
shabby, dust-covered lobby. They stood
silent, glancing over the withered deer heads
and faded lithographs suspended from the
walls; the scratched tables and sagging chairs,
the threadbare carpeting that covered the floor.
An octagon shaped clock with Roman numerals
faced them from an opposite corner, its hands
locked at high noon, the pendulum motionless
on dead center.

Men had gathered near the back of the room,
and as Kyler touched them with his look, Tom
Tolliver wheeled abruptly and came forward.

"Glad you showed up . . . Was thinkin'
maybe you wouldn't."

"Said we'd be here," Kyler replied laconi-
cally, following the rancher back to where the
others waited. He glanced about.

Tolliver said, "Reckon first thing is to intro-
duce you two." He pointed to a squat man on
the extreme left. "That's Claude Hayman. Runs

35

the Lazy H. Next to him is Al Pritchard, of the Pitchfork outfit. Then comes Bill Denby, the Box D. Bill's wife is the schoolteacher here.

"This is Otto Schmidt. Calls his place the Wagonwheel. You ever get real hungry, drop by and have a meal with him . . . Be the best cookin' you ever tasted."

Schmidt's broad, beet-red face broke into a wide smile. "It iss welcome you are, anytime, Mr. Kyler. And Mr. Wasco . . ."

Tolliver was working hard at selling him on the proposition they intended to offer, Sam realized. Again he wondered what it was all about; the men were anxious—and the pay was unusually high.

"Fellow with the gray suit there is Sol Weil, one of our local merchants. Runs the general merchandise store. That's Rufe Eggert behind him. Got a saloon down the street. Then we have Dave Simon. He's the youngest and the newest around here. He's doing fine with his D-Bar-S spread—unless he runs into bad luck. Man with the white hat next to him is Pete Clark. Pete's Circle 7 is down in the south corner of the Strip."

Tolliver paused when he came to the last of the group, a sharp-faced, hard-eyed man with gray hair who sat forward in his chair, both hands hooked on the curved handle of a cane.

"This is Shinn Thompson. Owns Spade—the biggest ranch in the country. And the oldest."

Unlike the others Thompson did not offer his hand, merely nodded. Tolliver turned to Kyler. "Not everybody's here. Charlie Kinsman, who owns the Palace, is out of town, and there's a couple of ranchers who couldn't make it, but I guess you could say this is a pretty representative bunch."

Blunt and to the point, Thompson said, "You lookin' for a job?"

Equally blunt, Kyler shrugged, answered, "Got a job. But I told Tolliver I'd hear you out. What's the deal?"

Tolliver motioned to a worn, leather covered couch. "Sit down . . . Both of you . . . Be easier listenin' . . ."

Wasco sank gratefully onto the hard cushion. Kyler settled beside him. Taking his money belt from his shoulder, he laid it across his lap, then stood the shotgun between his knees.

"Expect you know where you are," the rancher began. "Some call it the High Plains country, some say the Strip. Others call it

37

No-Man's-Land—and that's just what it is in more ways than one.

"There's five thousand square miles of fine land here that's not claimed by any of the surrounding states or territories. Nobody wants it—so we're stuck out here by ourselves. Not so bad in some ways, but it's got its drawbacks, too—main one being the law—or the lack of it."

Kyler nodded. He had already discovered the town had no marshal or sheriff. He hadn't realized, however, that the entire Strip was without protection.

"Result is the country's overrun by outlaws. Every gunslinger on the dodge heads for here because a lawman can't touch him, once he's inside the Strip. Even a US Marshal has no authority. You can see what sort of problems that creates."

"Kind of got an idea from the lady over in the restaurant," Kyler said.

"Marcia Ashwick? She could tell you about the town's side of it. Same as Sol or Rufe, here."

"They get us ranchers goin' and comin'," Bill Denby said.

"That's for sure," Pritchard of the Pitchfork

spread added. "They just set back and get fat collecting on every head of stock we send to market. . . . Two years ago they got it all."

Sam Kyler frowned. "How?"

"There's several gangs running loose around here. When we start the drive to market— Dalhart—two or three bunches join up and wait for us somewhere between here and the Texas line. Never the same place but they're always careful to be inside the Strip. They move in on the herd and either we pay cash—fifty cents a head it was last year—or they take enough beef to make up the amount. Road tax they call it."

"And you always fork over?" Wasco asked in a disbelieving voice.

Dave Simon stirred. "What the hell can we do? Usually fifteen or twenty of them—all hard-case gunmen. We've got maybe ten riders pushing the herd, none of them a match for the gunslingers. Be the same story if we had twenty riders. We couldn't buck them."

"Be damn fools if we tried," Denby said.

"And that ain't all," Shinn Thompson said. "Year before last they ambushed the crew on the way back from Dalhart. Wasn't the same gang, so the boys said. Robbed them of the

39

money we got for the herd. Tried it last year but the boys outrun 'em."

"Sure to try again this year," Pete Clark said gloomily. "If they do, they'll flat bust me . . ."

"Includes all of us," Denby said. "Ain't got over my losses from that deal two years ago, yet. Same goes for the town. We go broke; the town goes broke."

"Got the idea you've had a lawman around."

"Tried, but we've never found the right man," Tolliver said, and hesitated. "I'll be honest with you, Kyler. These gangs are tough —toughest you've ever come up against, I expect. The worst men from all over the country have drifted in here."

"You ever think of calling in the army?"

"Half a dozen times. They ignore us. We heard in a round-about way the government was afraid the soldiers would rile the Indians—us being just west of Indian Territory. Politicians therefore only look the other way when we holler—make out like we wasn't even here."

Sam Kyler rubbed at the round ends of the shotgun's barrel. "So I take from what you're telling me you want to hire Wasco and me to get your herd through to Dalhart without paying off—and then get your money back safe to you."

Tolliver nodded. "We figure if it can be done, you're the man who can do it."

Shinn Thompson snorted. "It's a damn fool idea! One man and a helper ain't goin' to get the job done—no matter who or what he is."

Kyler shifted his eyes to the old rancher. "You mean I—we do it alone?"

"How else? Sure you'll have our drovers with you. Ordinary ranch hands—but they're a hell of a long ways from being gunfighters. Wouldn't be no use to you in a shootout. Only get themselves killed."

Sam glanced at Wasco, turned to Tolliver. "How many ranches on the Strip?"

"Nine."

"Two men from each, we—"

"Mace Buckman's place ain't workin' right now," Pete Clark said. "Got to figure on eight."

"Buckman's in the pen," Thompson broke in. "For murderin' my son—"

"Kyler's not interested in that," Tolliver said quickly, closing what was evidently a sore subject before it could get started. "Sure . . . We can spare you two men from each of our spreads . . . Sixteen riders. But like Shinn said,

41

they won't be of any help when it comes to gunplay. They're just cowhands."

"How about you men?"

Simon, his eyes snapping, said, "Count me in, by God!"

Tolliver wagged his head. "Don't be a fool, Dave. You're in the same wagon as the rest of us. We can all shoot a gun but we'd be in way over our heads taking on those outlaws. Smart thing for us to do is leave it to a professional— like Kyler."

Silence fell over the lobby. Sam continued to rub at the shotgun's muzzle, his eyes half-closed. Finally, he said, "Be quite a chore . . . Ever think of hiring outriders in Dalhart?"

"Tried to," Shinn Thompson said. "Nobody willing to take on the gangs."

"How long before the herd's ready to move?"

"Time's run out. Gather's begun and the stock's due at the loading pens by the end of this week."

Kyler nodded. "One thing more. What kind of money you willing to pay?"

Tolliver rose to his feet. "Talked it over while we were waiting. We'll ante up five hundred for you—two-fifty for your friend there. In gold.

42

We've got to make it this year or, like Pete Clark said, we're all broke."

"But we're only payin' off if you get the stock through without turnin' over part of it to the outlaws—and get back with the money," Shinn Thompson warned.

Kyler signified his understanding. Five hundred in gold. It was a lot of money. He would still have plenty left after making up the shortage in Arch Clayborn's money belt. But it would be one hell of a job. He turned to Wasco.

"What do you think?"

The old puncher rubbed at his chin. "Well, I sure ain't buckin' for no real estate in a graveyard, but if you say so, I reckon I'm willin'."

Sam Kyler looked up at Tolliver. "All right. You've got yourself a deal."

6

OTTO SCHMIDT heaved a deep sigh. Shinn Thompson shook his head. Bill Denby came to his feet, extended his hand to Kyler.

"Want you to know how much this means to us—all of us."

"Not over with yet," Sam said.

"He's right," Thompson broke in. "I still figure it's a fool deal. You're bankin' everything on the reputation of one man—and I ain't yet seen a reputation stop a bullet."

Tolliver said, "That's so—but at least we've found a man who's willing to try."

"Tryin' ain't doin'," Thompson countered stubbornly. "Better save your back pattin' until later."

Kyler grinned wryly. The old rancher was right. The job was a long way from being accomplished—and the odds for success were poor. But in the back of his mind a plan was shaping up. If he could split the gang . . .

"Couple of things I want to get straight," he said.

Tolliver nodded. "Shoot."

"You told me the outlaws took cattle in payment. How do they get rid of them?"

"Sell them in Dalhart or some other rail-head."

"How can they get away with that? The beef's stolen."

"They force us to give them a bill of sale. We always carry a few blanks so we can list the right tally once the drive's over."

"Sure a brassy bunch," Wasco commented.

"Can afford to be," Denby said. "They got it all their way."

"Know anything about the gang—who they are, I mean?"

"Not always the same bunch, except for the head man. Name's Eli Hurd. He's plenty smart and knows all the angles. Ever hear of him?"

Kyler shook his head. "It's settled then. We can figure on each of you furnishing us with two riders—all good cowpunchers who can handle a herd."

"Count me in, too," Dave Simon said. "And Pritchard's willing—"

"No," Kyler broke in. "I'd as soon you

owners would stay out of it. Give me your best hands—that's all I need."

A sudden silence descended over the room. Shinn Thompson finally said, "Now, why the hell don't you want—"

"If I'm to ramrod this drive, I want it done my way. Don't figure to have somebody second-guessing me if I make up my mind to do something."

Claude Hayman, quiet up to that point, said, "Makes sense. We're saddlin' the man with one hell of a chore. Let him do it the way he wants."

Tolliver glanced around the circle of men. "Agreed?"

They all nodded. Sam Kyler said, "Then have your riders and your herd at the gathering place—"

"Skull Canyon—"

"At Skull Canyon ready to move out by sundown tomorrow. Won't actually start the drive until the next morning, but I want everything set. That possible?"

Tolliver said, "No trouble. About all the cattle's there now. Think Denby's stuff is still due—"

"Boys are driving my herd in now . . .

Expect they'll have them bedded down by dark," Denby said.

"How long will it take to reach Dalhart?"

"Three days, more or less. Easy going— mostly flat land and shallow draws, route we follow."

"Any water?"

"Rifle Creek. You'll hit it just before you come to the Texas line."

"How about extra horses and a chuck wagon?"

"All taken care of."

"Good. No need for us to bother about details."

"Nope. We'll see to everything. All you got to worry about is getting through—and back."

"Which won't be no picnic," Shinn Thompson said and pointed with his cane at the window. "Wolves are already beginnin' to gather."

Kyler rose, looked through the dust-streaked glass fronting the Fargo's lobby. Six riders were moving slowly down the street. All were tough, belted men.

"Headed for your place, Rufe," Denby said.

Eggert, somewhat aside and in conversation

47

with Tom Tolliver, moved quickly to Kyler's side. He gave the men a close speculation.

"Strangers to me," he said after a moment. "Reckon I'd better be gettin' over there."

Wheeling abruptly, he crossed to the door and entered the street. Shinn Thompson hawked, spat at a brass cuspidor.

"Be some hell around here tonight."

Kyler came back around. None of the six men were familiar to him—but he recognized the stamp. They would be the sort he would be up against on the drive.

"There only one trail out of here to Dalhart?" Tolliver said. "Only one that's practical. You swing east or west, you hit bad country . . . Outlaws would head you off, anyway."

"Never heard nobody mention it," Wasco said. "Just how big a herd you movin'?"

"Three thousand head."

The old puncher whistled softly. "Handlin' them alone's a sight of a chore without worryin' about them fancy rustlers!"

"That bunch didn't stay long at Rufe's," Denby remarked, peering through the window. "Headin' into Marcia's place now."

Kyler wheeled, placed his glance on the swaggering figures entering the restaurant. As he watched, one of the men paused, raised his foot and deliberately kicked one of the tables, sent it skittering into the others. Suddenly angry, Sam Kyler turned to Wasco.

"Let's go get a cup of coffee," he said, and started for the door.

"Hold on a minute," Claude Hayman cut in as the old puncher got to his feet. "Let the widow look out for herself. You're workin' for us."

"Way I see it," Kyler replied coolly, "is we're working for everybody around here . . . And right now's a good time to start."

7

WHEN they reached the entrance to Marcia Ashwick's restaurant Kyler halted, motioned to Wasco for silence. Inside the outlaws had taken over, were sprawled about on chairs scattered throughout the room. One, a squat, dark man with a pock-marked face, had placed one booted foot against the short counter and was rocking it back and forth. Dishes were rattling noisily and a sugar bowl had already crashed to the floor, spilled its contents.

Marcia Ashwick stood defiantly before the outlaw. "Get out!" she said in a firm voice. "I won't serve you!"

"You sure better, lady," the scarred man replied, "unless you want me and the boys to just help ourselves." He glanced around at the grinning features of his friends. "Reckon I ought to tell you, howsomever, we ain't so handy in a place like this. Doubt if it'd look like much once we was through. . . ."

Marcia shook her head in helpless anger. "Do

what you like—I can't stop you! But I won't serve you. Last time you were in here you refused to pay. I—I'd rather be out of business than put up with—"

"Guess that means we got to help ourselves," the outlaw cut in and gave the counter a final, hard shove. It went over backwards, spilling dishes off its surface, dumping various supplies from its shelves.

Sam Kyler stepped through the doorway. Wasco followed, halted just inside, long arms folded across his chest. Kyler moved straight to the pock-marked outlaw, seized him by the collar and dragged him to his feet. The man yelled, jerked free and whirled.

"Who the hell you think you are—"

"I'm the man who's going to make you pay for all this damage," Sam replied in a tight voice. "Shell out!"

"Nobody's makin' me do—"

Kyler lashed out with the shotgun. The barrel caught the outlaw across the side of his head, sent him staggering against the wall. The others leaped to their feet. Wasco's flat, nasal voice froze them in their tracks.

"Just stand easy, boys . . . And don't go

51

reachin' for them hoglegs unless'n you want daylight shinin' through your hides."

The squat outlaw rubbed at the side of his head, glared at Kyler. For a brief moment he considered going for his gun, then thought better of it.

"You ain't got no call—"

"Dig out your money," Kyler snapped. He shifted his glance to Marcie Ashwick. White faced, she had drawn back against the partition that separated the kitchen from the dining area. "Twenty dollars cover it?"

She nodded hurriedly. Sam swung back to the outlaw. "Fork it over!"

The scarred man shook his head. "I ain't got twenty dollars—"

"Then call on your friends."

The outlaw looked expectantly toward his companions. All reached for their pockets.

"Watch them hands!" Wasco shouted. He was holding two guns, his own ancient weapon and the one taken from Shad Collins. "Sure would hate to kill a man just 'cause he made a mistake!"

When the necessary amount had been accumulated and turned over to Marcia

52

Ashwick, Kyler stepped back to the side of the old puncher. He motioned with the shotgun.

"Now we'll straighten things up a bit. Set that counter up the way it belongs . . . And put those tables and chairs back like you found them."

Grumbling, the outlaws did as they were ordered. Finished, they moved toward the door. Kyler halted them.

"One thing more. If you ever come in here again and pull a stunt like that—or refuse to pay for your meal—I'll run you down and blow your head off . . . That's a promise."

The pock-marked outlaw stared. "For one lousy four-bit meal?"

"For just one cup of coffee . . . All the same . . . Now get out—and if you'd like to talk about this some more, you'll find us around."

The men trooped out into the street. Halfway across they slowed, looked back, and then continued on in the direction of Rufe Eggert's.

Marcia Ashwick's eyes were shining. She came forward. "I—I don't know how to thank you . . ."

"No need," Kyler said.

"No need!" she echoed. "We've been needing someone around here for a long time

53

to handle men like those—somebody to put them in their place. You're the first to even try."

"Had plenty of help," Kyler said, grinning at Wasco. "Don't think anybody's going to argue with him and all that hardware he's packin'."

"When the town hears this—"

"No point in mentioning it. Besides, we'll be gone."

"Gone! Then you are going to work for the cattlemen."

Kyler nodded. "Driving a herd through to Dalhart."

"And fighting off twenty or thirty outlaws doing so. Oh—I knew they would talk you into it."

"We're getting paid. Plenty."

"But you'll never live to spend it. Not if you do what they want you to. Tell them you've changed your mind. Stay here—take the marshal's job. At least the odds for keeping alive are better."

Kyler smiled. "Man stops to figure the odds, he never gets anything done. We'll make it. Don't worry about it."

Marcia Ashwick sighed resignedly. "I knew

it was too much to hope for." She drew herself up, smiled. "At least you can let me serve you a fine supper for what you've done for me."

Sam glanced at Wasco. "Appreciate the invitation. We need to clean up a mite. Offer hold good a couple hours from now?"

"Of course."

"Then we'll check in at the hotel and come back later."

"Is that a promise?"

"You can bet on it," Kyler said, and started for the door.

8

THE afternoon of the next day, Kyler and Wasco, after getting directions from Sol Weil, rode into the broad, steep walled defile known as Skull Canyon. A heavy pall of yellow dust hung over the area and the air was filled with the sounds of bawling cattle and shouting men.

They drew to a halt on the northern lip of the natural corral and looked for signs of the camp. Riders were wheeling in and out of the confusion but it was several minutes before they finally spotted the canvas topped chuck wagon halted at the far end of the canyon where dust was at a minimum.

As they moved on, riding down a long slope, Wasco twisted about on his saddle. "We ain't done much palaverin' about this here fandango —and way it stacks up, appears we bit ourselves off quite a chaw. You got some special ideas how we can do it?"

Kyler shook his head. "Start the drive—see what happens. Little hard to make any plans yet."

"Reckon you ain't forgot that if it comes down to shootin', it'll be just you and me. Them cow-nurses ain't goin' to be no help."

"Big reason why we've got to dodge a show-down, if we can."

"Yeh—if we can," Wasco said morosely. "I figure them owlhoots'll have plenty to say about that."

They found most of the ranchers at the wagon hunched on their heels drinking black coffee from tin cups as they watched the final activities of the gather. When they rode in Dave Simon greeted them.

"Step down . . . Plenty java there on the fire."

Kyler and Wasco anchored their horses to the picket line and returned to the wagon.

"About set," Pritchard said, smiling at Sam.

Kyler nodded, poured coffee for Wasco and himself. A man came from the interior of the wagon where he was arranging supplies, grinned.

"Howdy. Name's Turkey. I'm your cook."

Kyler pressed the oldster's horny hand, turned to the ranchers. Shinn Thompson and Schmidt were absent, he noticed.

"Like we figure—right at three thousand

head," Tolliver said, thrusting a sheaf of papers upon which he had been figuring back into his pocket. "Biggest tally we ever had." He hesitated, frowned. "Maybe that ain't so good. We could only scare up twelve riders for you."

A thread of impatience stirred through Kyler as he studied the mass of shifting bodies. He would be short-handed—and that wasn't good.

"Getting this stock through is pretty important to you. Seems you could find the men somewhere."

Pritchard swore softly. "Everything's wrong this year. And you've got to understand none of us are very big as ranchers go. Exceptin' Thompson, pulling two men off leaves a big hole. On top of that there's two or three down sick, and one of Clark's boys got throwed yesterday and broke his arm. . . ."

Billy Denby nodded. "Something else you maybe won't be likin'. I got only two hired hands. Can't spare either one so it'll be me riding from my outfit."

Sam raised his cup to his lips, slowly drained its contents. They would be starting the drive short of drovers—and with one of the owners along. They would be lucky to maintain control of the herd, if anything went wrong, much less do anything about the outlaws. From behind him Wasco's laconic voice broke the quiet.

"Was we smart, we'd forget this here jack-screw deal 'fore we even start."

Tolliver's leathery face showed instant alarm. "Now, hold on a minute! We know you laid down your conditions, hard and fast, and we figured you had your reasons. But we just couldn't do it exactly like you wanted. You got to see our side of it, too."

"It's your beef," Sam reminded the rancher.

"Realize that, but there ain't none of us in shape to just turn loose all holds. We got our ranches to look after, too . . . Don't mean selling our cattle's not important, just that there's other things we got to look out for."

"And if it's me comin' along that's botherin' you," Denby said, "I ain't doin' it because I want to. It's because I have to. It's either me from my place—or nobody."

"Bill's give us his word he won't give you any trouble," Claude Hayman said.

Denby nodded vigorously. "You're the trail boss, Kyler. Whatever you say goes."

Sam considered throughtfully, finally shrugged. "All right, we'll do the best we can," he said, and then added to Denby, "I'll hold you to your word. You're just one of the drovers until we get back. Went on a drive once with the owner of the stock hanging around my neck. Don't aim to let it happen again."

"You've got my hand on it," Denby said, his face serious.

Tolliver's features showed his relief. He took a leather fold from his pocket, drew Kyler aside beyond hearing of the other men.

"Here's your papers—bills of sale and such. May have to change the tally sheet when you get to the pens, depending on the kind of luck you have."

"Won't lose any stock unless we're so short of men we can't hold them," Sam answered.

"That happens you won't be responsible. We'll understand. One other thing. Coming back with the money you might try swinging west, keeping off the main trail. Rough country, no good for driving cattle but a man on horseback can manage it easy. Could be a way to dodge the outlaws. Chances are they'll be layin' their ambush on the regular route."

"Good idea," Kyler said. "Where do I hit it?"

"About five miles west. Trail follows along a

with two heads . . . Reckon it ain't only the outlaws that are goin' to be givin' us trouble."

"Denby's a good man," Kyler said quietly. "But he's got some learning to do."

9

THE moaning of the wind awoke Sam Kyler. He sat up in the half darkness, flinched as sand blasted against his face, stung his eyes. He and Wasco had chosen a place just beyond the chuck wagon to spread their bedrolls and they were now lying unprotected against the gusts. A loud slapping sound drew his attention. He turned about, saw the angular shape of Turkey struggling to tie down the canvas top of his vehicle before it could be whirled away.

Kyler scrambled to his feet, prodding Wasco awake in the process. Hanging tight to his blankets, he made his way to the comparative calm behind the wagon, the old puncher muttering curses and spitting sand a step to his left.

"For chrissake—somebody . . . Give me a hand here!"

Turkey's strained voice carried faintly to them and throwing their bedrolls into the wagon, both turned to where the cook was clinging desperately to a corner of the wildly flapping fabric. Sam grabbed a loose rope, poked it through the metal eye at the end of the wagonbed, cinched it down as Wasco gave his support to Turkey.

"Obliged!" the cook shouted above the howl of the storm. "Dang thing come loose somehow . . . Sure is a bad one."

Kyler nodded, yelled to Wasco. "Turn the crew out. Tell them to meet me at the herd."

The old puncher bobbed his head as Kyler wheeled and moved to the picket line. He saddled the bay, taking time to check the other horses, and then swung back for the center of the canyon where the cattle were gathered. Darkness and swirling sand and dust made it impossible to see any distance, and he heard the sounds of the restless brutes several moments before he was upon them.

The windstorm had aroused them and they were beginning to shift nervously. Sam, riding in close, saw the shadowy outlines of the men delegated to night watch, moving slowly along the fringe of the herd, doing what they could to quiet the stock. A puncher loomed up before him. It was one of Pritchard's men. He pulled up short when he saw Kyler, a startled look on his face. He brushed the grit from his mouth, rode in close.

"Won't take much to spook these critters!" he yelled. A fresh blast of sand struck him. He swore, again sleeved his lips.

Kyler glanced to the east. Through the heavy pall he could see the first gray hint of daylight. He spurred the bay nearer to the rider.

"They start milling, get in behind and start pushing them south . . . I'll pass the word."

Pritchard's man wheeled away and was swallowed immediately by the dust. Sam moved forward, halted again as Wasco, leading the balance of the crew, loped up. He repeated his orders.

"If you don't watch close, the herd will start drifting with the storm—north—soon as it's light. Got to keep them from it. One of you double back and tell Turkey to pull out. Have to eat later—when we get a chance."

The riders loped off. Wasco fought his horse in closer to Kyler. "Anythin' special you want me doin'?"

Sam shook his head. "Just keep them from breaking loose and heading north."

Wasco angled off into the murk and Kyler rode in nearer to the stirring cattle, seeking the remainder of the crew. Unless they maintained a close watch the herd would soon start breaking up, form into small bunches that would be difficult to contain. In the blinding storm they would scatter to all directions.

He found most of the riders patrolling close to the nervous cattle, doing their utmost to keep the calm. But as the light grew stronger, the herd became increasingly hard to handle. Finally, with the land about them distinct, the cattle began to move. Here and there a steer would break from the main body, plunge off into the brash. A puncher would immediately swing out after him, haze him back with his rope.

Bill Denby, his face strained his mouth and eyes rimmed with sand, rode up.

"Ain't goin' to hold them much longer!" he shouted above the whining wind.

"No need!" Sam yelled his reply. "Head 'em out—down the draw."

Denby nodded and whirled away, motioning to the drovers as he loped by. Wasco appeared and Kyler pointed toward the south. The old puncher waved and cut back into the dust.

In only moments the herd began to move, shifting uncertainly back and forth at first but finally, after a fair sized jag of the stock had moved into the wide, shallow wash at the south end of the canyon, all fell into a heaving, bawling procession.

Kyler, circling the flowing mass, kept his drovers in tight. Once the herd was well underway, the job would not be so difficult; it would be only a matter of keeping it pointed in the right direction.

In the draw they were partly shielded from the blustering wind, and for an hour the cattle plodded along with little urging. Then, when they broke out onto a high flat and once more were heading straight into the teeth of the storm, trouble immediately developed.

The drive began to stall. Cattle started milling, sought to turn, put their hindquarters to the stinging gusts. Kyler, aided by Wasco and the drovers, hammered at them ceaselessly, but progress came almost to a standstill.

Dawn broke over a swirling, choked world and Sam's hope for a cessation of the fierce wind at the arrival of daylight, faded. He considered calling a halt, decided against it. Keeping the herd intact, once stopped, would be too difficult; better to keep it moving, however slow.

They overtook the chuck wagon a short time later. Turkey had coffee and fried meat ready and the men took turns, two at a time, to have a quick, if gritty meal.

The morning wore on with no let-up in the storm or the hard labor. The riders changed horses and Kyler forsook his worn bay for a chunky little buckskin that had no liking for him or the storm either and continually fought the bit.

Around noon the wind began to decrease. The herd became less difficult to manage but Kyler knew this was only temporary. The driving storm had dried out the stock, turned them thirsty well before time. They would soon turn impatient for water—and Rifle Creek was still a day or more distant.

Plagued with this new problem, Sam pulled away from his position in front of the herd and drew off to one side. Wasco and Denby were riding point while the remainder of the crew were scattered along at swing and drag positions. Dust hovered above the slow moving herd in a vast cloud and he could see neither the far side nor the rear.

Hailing the first drover who appeared in the dry boil, Kyler beckoned to him. The man was an oldster, one of Shinn Thompson's hands. His brows were thick with sand and when he pulled down the bandanna he had drawn across the lower half of his face, it looked as though he wore a mask.

He grinned at Sam. "One hell of a lot of real estate on the move around here!"

Kyler smiled back. "For a fact . . . Any water closer than Rifle Creek?"

The puncher scratched at his ear, thought for a moment. "Nope, not unless you swing east . . . Reckon it'd be about twenty miles."

Sam considered that. A full day's drive. There was no point in forsaking the regular trail; they would reach Rifle Creek and the usual water stop sooner if they continued on.

"Thinkin' about changin'?"

Kyler shook his head. "Be nothing gained."

The rider signified his agreement, commented again on the storm, and dropped back to his position with the herd. They pushed on, the cattle growing more recalcitrant with the tedious miles, and when darkness finally came, Kyler welcomed the halt. He chose a broad depression between three low lying hills for night camp. It wasn't the best place to bed down three thousand and thirty beefs, but he had earlier scouted ahead with Wasco and found nothing more suitable.

Taking no chances, he assigned half the crew to stand watch and sent the rest in for their evening meal. When they had finished they relieved the others who ate then settled back for a few hours rest. At midnight they would spell the first nighthawks.

Kyler was finishing off his second cup of coffee when Bill Denby, haggard and scoured raw by sand, came in. It was the first Sam had seen of the rancher, except for fleeting glimpses, since the storm began. Denby accepted his plate of meat and biscuits from the cook and squatted on his heels.

"We're in for hell if that wind gets up again tonight," he said wearily.

"For sure," Kyler replied. "One thing in our favor. Cattle are dead beat. They won't be so anxious to run . . . How far are we from Rifle Creek?"

Denby stared off across the darkening flats to a scatter of hills in the south. "Ought to reach it by tomorrow noon, figurin' we don't have trouble."

"Something we've got to walk around. If they

get stirred up again, do what we did this morning—head them south and let 'em go."

"Temper they're in now, it maybe won't work."

Kyler rose, helped himself to more coffee. "We'll make it work. If that herd ever busts up we'll be all summer rounding up the strays."

Denby shrugged gloomily. "Seems to me like this was a hard luck drive right from the start."

But the night passed without incident and at daylight the herd was again on the move, rested although pushed by thirst. Where, that previous day it had been the wind and slashing sand that made them difficult to handle, the need for water was now the threatening factor.

The crew, under the supervision of trail-wise old Wasco, handled them well, however, and the stock moved steadily southward at a fair pace. Around midday Bill Denby caught up with Kyler. He wheeled in alongside, pointed to a fall of land a mile or so on ahead.

"Creek's there," he said. "Cattle are gettin' wind of it now. They're startin' to perk up."

Kyler breathed a sigh. Maybe the worst of the drive would be over once the herd slaked its thirst. He rode on with Denby, leaving behind the herd which had now broken into a shambling trot. The two men reached the last, gradual slope, topped out the rise and dropped over onto the opposing side. The bright sparkle of a broad stream cutting a path along the floor of the valley greeted them.

And there was something else: outlaws.

10

DENBY pulled to a quick halt. "Just like before," he said in a taut voice. "Settin' and waitin' for us."

Sam Kyler's eyes were on the outlaws. There were fifteen in the gang. They had drawn up in a line at the foot of the slope with Rifle Creek a few yards behind them.

"What're you aimin' to do?" Denby asked.

Kyler shook his head. There was the quick drumming of a running horse back of him and a moment later Wasco pulled up at his side. The old puncher whistled softly.

"Looks like they're gettin' ready for a cavalry charge . . ."

"What are we goin' to do?" Denby asked again.

Kyler shifted his glance to the rancher. "We take things as they come. Whatever—stay out of it. Leave it to me."

Denby said, "Sure . . . sure."

Kyler touched the bay with his spurs and with Wasco to his left, the rancher on his right, rode in close to the waiting men. Faint surprise ran through him when he saw Shad Collins near the end of the line. The young outlaw eyed him narrowly, equally startled.

"This the same bunch that jumped you last year?"

"Don't know." Denby replied. "Wasn't along, but it probably is. Same head man—one in the middle there with the checked vest. That's Eli Hurd."

Sam moved forward a few more paces, studying the outlaw chief. The man's dark, hard cornered face struck no chords in his memory. A few of his followers did, however. They returned his stare sullenly. Near enough Kyler again halted.

Before he could speak, Hurd said: "You the ramrod of this outfit?"

"That's me," Sam answered.

From down the line Shad Collins volunteered, "He's Sam Kyler, Eli. Reckon you've heard of him."

Hurd's eyes flared slightly. After a moment, he said "Shotgun Sam Kyler . . . Yeh, I've heard of him." Then, "We're here for our cut. Expect you know about it."

"I know one thing," Sam replied coolly.

"You better get the hell away from the front of that creek. There's a herd of beef coming over that ridge in about five minutes—all in a hurry to get a drink."

Eli Hurd opened his mouth to make some sort of answer, then paused as the low thunder of hooves reached him. Not waiting to see what the outlaws would do, Kyler wheeled, and with Wasco and Denby close behind, loped off to one side.

The outlaws followed hastily, some with drawn weapons, as though suspecting trickery, others interested only in getting out of the way.

The forerunners of the herd broke over the rim at that moment, started down the slope bawling loudly. Seconds later the remainder of the cattle appeared and a solid wave of brown, white and black surged over the crest, flowed down to the stream and began to split and spread out along the water.

The crew, bringing up the rear, halted on the ridge. After a moment they cut diagonally across the slope and took up positions in a half-circle behind Kyler.

Eli Hurd moved out a stride in front of his men. All of the outlaws had pulled their weapons upon the arrival of the crew and now watched intently. Kyler gave them a swift but thorough study, calculating his chances. It was as he had been told; all were tough, hardened gunmen. He understood better why the ranchers were unwilling to fight. Pitting ordinary cowhands against such killers would mean nothing short of wholesale slaughter.

"Let's get this over with," Hurd said. "You got your papers?"

Anger stirred through Kyler. The thought of being forced to knuckle under and accede to the outlaw's demands rankled him. "What are you talking about?"

Eli Hurd spat. "Don't give me that. You've been told. The pay-off in cash or cattle?"

"We don't carry any cash," Bill Denby said.

The outlaw considered the rancher coldly. "All right, I'll take cattle."

"How many?" Kyler asked, slanting a warning look at Denby.

"Dollar a head."

"A dollar!" Denby shouted. "Last year was only fifty cents! By God—I'll see you in hell—".

"Taxes has gone up," Hurd cut in quietly. The half-smile faded from his lips. "Now, if you're aimin' to argue about it—I got me some real good collectors along."

"He's not running this drive," Kyler broke in quickly. "You're dealing with me."

He watched the men beyond Hurd settle back gently, breathed deeper. It had been a dangerous moment. One false move on the part of the drovers and violence would have erupted.

"Then do the talkin'," Hurd said. "How many head you driving?"

"Three thousand."

Hurd twisted about in his saddle, directed himself to one of his men. "Engle, Mister Kyler says he's got three thousand head. That what you make it?"

The outlaw wheeled about, rode a short distance toward the herd and stopped. He surveyed the watering stock for a long minute, then rejoined the line.

"What I figure," he said.

Hurd nodded. "Engle used to be a cattleman," he said. "Knows his critters. Never knew him to miss a tally more'n a dozen or so."

Kyler said nothing, leaving it up to the outlaw to make the next move. To fight was out of the question, and he was giving that course of action no consideration. A vague plan had occurred to him that seemed best, and to accomplish it he should simply lay back, let Eli

Hurd have his way for the time being. His biggest worry was that Denby, or one of the drovers, would lose his head, do something foolish.

"Three thousand . . ." Hurd said, frowning. "Means my cut'll be two hundred head. Hear they're paying fifteen dollars for prime steers in Dalhart. That how you calculate it, Mister Kyler?"

"That's what it figures."

Sam reached down unbuckled his left-hand saddlebag, procured the leather fold of papers. A low muttering arose among the drovers. Denby swore. Kyler gave them a warning look, passed a blank bill of sale to the rancher.

"Fill it out," he ordered. "And don't try anything stupid."

11

DENBY snatched the sheet from Kyler's fingers. There was a sudden stir among the drovers. Sam turned sharply. Andy, one of the younger riders, pushed forward, his hand resting on the butt of his pistol. The boy's face was taut and his eyes blazed.

"I figure it's about time we done somethin' about this!" he muttered.

"Back up!" Kyler snapped.

He glanced over his shoulder at the line of outlaws. They were watching, waiting quietly, alert for any opposition.

Wasco reached out, laid his hand on the boy's shoulder. "Simmer down, youngster."

Andy shrugged the old puncher off. "Was a mistake hirin' him. Could be this is all a put-up job."

Anger rolled through Kyler. Wasco glanced up hurriedly, wagged his head. "Reckon he didn't mean that, Sam. Just shootin' off his mouth. Got to remember he's still a mite wet-eared."

"You ain't talkin' for me," the boy shot back.

"Dry up, Andy," one of the drovers cut in. "Maybe none of us goes along with this here doin's, but Kyler's runnin' it. Let him do what he wants—he's the one that's got to do the explainin' when we get home."

"Here—" Bill Denby said abruptly, holding out the sheet of paper to Kyler. "Here's your damned bill of sale . . ."

Kyler accepted it, glanced briefly at the writing, then rode toward Eli Hurd. Several of the outlaws came to attention at his approach. Hurd laughed.

"Ease off, boys . . . Mister Kyler ain't no hero."

Sam, his mouth a hard line, halted before the outlaw leader and passed over the paper.

"We'll cut 'em out," Hurd said, thrusting the bill of sale into his vest pocket. "Be taking them off the end."

"Two hundred head," Kyler said. "No more."

Again Hurd laughed. "Sure. This here's a business deal—pure business. I don't aim to cheat nobody."

Under his breath Bill Denby said, "Hell of a lot of good it done to hire this Kyler. We could've just forked over the stock without him."

"Reckon he's doin' what's best," Wasco replied.

"Doin'!" the rancher said bitterly. "He ain't doin' nothin'! . . . And we was all hopin' he'd put an end to this rustlin'."

"Last verse of the song ain't sung yet," the old puncher murmured. "Just set quiet and keep your lip buttoned. Sam ain't likin' this no more'n you, but he ain't lookin' to spill no blood."

"'Specially his," young Andy commented acidly.

Wasco turned, stared closely at the boy. "How'd you grow old as you are? Sure don't hardly seem possible."

"I can take care of myself," the puncher mumbled.

"Misdoubt that," Wasco said. "Leastwise, for not much longer."

Kyler, watching Hurd and part of his men turn away while anger slowly consumed him, wheeled finally to the drovers.

"One hour and we move on," he snapped. "Want to be over the Texas line by dark."

Immediately Bill Denby frowned. "No hurry now . . . Besides, stock ought to water good—"

"Goddammit!" Kyler shouted, unable to contain his temper. "You heard me!"

Behind him the outlaws, left by Hurd, watched and waited. The promise of violence still hung over the two groups of men like a threatening cloud. Kyler realized he must end the confrontation as quickly as possible before a spark could set off an explosion.

"All right!" he barked. "You've got no time to sit there. Get over to the wagon and eat. You won't have another chance until night."

For a long minute the riders made no move to comply and then Bill Denby pulled out of the silent men.

"Come on," he said in a stiff, angry way. "Do what he says."

The drovers turned, rode slowly by Kyler. Wasco paused, looked questioningly at Sam.

"Keep them close to camp," Kyler said. "This thing's not over yet."

The old puncher nodded and followed the others on to the chuck wagon. When they had dismounted, he swung the bay about and headed for the crown of the hill fronting the creek. From that point he could look down upon the activities.

Immediately, four of Hurd's men pulled out of the line, angled to where they could watch Kyler. Hurd himself wheeled around and rode down to join the party hazing his two hundred steers from the main herd.

A half dozen more beefs broke from the larger body, began to follow those cut out by the outlaws. Eli Hurd paused, glanced uphill to where Kyler sat. He grinned broadly, deliberately rode in behind the small jag and drove them into the ranks of those being taken.

Kyler's mouth twisted into a hard smile. The outlaws were holding the whip at the moment —but it wouldn't be for long.

Over at the chuck wagon one of the crew, noticing the theft, lunged to his feet, shouted, "Hey—you bunch of damned—" In the next moment Wasco had the man by the arm and was dragging him back.

Again Eli Hurd looked toward Kyler, the smile still on his dark face. He lifted his hand in mock salutation and joined his riders, now moving their herd out of the hollow. The few men remained in the line watching the drovers, wheeled about, loped off in pursuit. As they passed, the quartette keeping a watchful eye on Sam pulled off with them.

All rose to overtake Hurd; one paused, removing his hat and held it aloft. "Solong, Mister Shotgun," he called in a loud voice. "Was real pleasured to meet you!"

His companions laughed. Another shouted something additional, but the words were lost to Kyler. He shifted his gaze to the chuck wagon. The drovers were watching him closely, taking it all in—and wondering.

They expected him to do something, he realized. And he would welcome the opportunity; they couldn't know how much he would like to open up on the outlaws, wipe the smirks from their whiskered faces. But it was not the time or the place. To start something would result in massacre. He could do nothing but hold his peace regardless of what the crew thought of him.

He watched Eli Hurd and his men until they were over the ridge and out of sight. They were pointing due east where lay the rough country; evidently they planned to swing wide and enter Dalhart from that end. He considered this thoughtfully for a time, and then glancing at the sun, now sliding toward the western horizon, he returned to the wagon.

The drovers had finished their meal, were now sprawled about in the scanty shade glumly taking their ease. Kyler touched them with his eyes, jerked a thumb toward the herd.

"Move 'em out," he said crisply.

The men rose reluctantly, made their way to the horses and mounting, slanted for the herd. Wasco stepped up, bringing a tin cup of coffee and a thick meat and bread sandwich.

"Reckon I best keep proddin' them," he said, and sought out his own black.

Sam nodded his thanks and turned to watch. The cattle had satisfied their thirsts; most had drifted away from the creek, and were now grazing on the grass along the opposite bank. The crew had little trouble getting them started and in a short time they were plodding up the slope leading out of the valley.

Kyler finished his lunch, went back to the saddle and caught up with the drive. The herd gained the crest of the valley's southern slope, spilled out onto a broad plain. It was easy going and shortly before dark they crossed the Texas line and entered a long canyon. Kyler called a halt just as the sun's last rays began to fade.

When the stock had settled down and the night watches established, Sam signaled Wasco to his side.

"You're taking over," he said, handing the old puncher the fold of papers. "I'll meet you in Dalhart. The Longhorn Saloon."

Wasco peered at him through bushy brows. "What're you fixin' to do?"

"Going after those two hundred steers . . . We don't get paid unless we deliver them all. . . . Remember?"

"I remember . . . But you can't do it alone. Hell—they's fifteen of them—"

"I figure they'll split up. Hurd won't go riding into Dalhart with that many drovers for such a small bunch of cattle. Somebody'd get suspicious."

"Maybe. That Hurd strikes me as a feller who don't much care what anybody thinks. How about lettin' Denby take over so's I can trail along with you?"

"One of us has got to stay with the herd."

The old puncher sighed, shook his head. "All right. We'll do it your way."

Kyler started to pull off. Over his shoulder he said, "Be waiting for me at the Longhorn."

The old puncher nodded. "We'll be there. You just be dang sure you make it."

12

SAM KYLER cut a diagonal course to the northeast, reasoning that if the outlaws continued in the direction they had taken, he would eventually cross their path. That they had a long lead was undeniable; it had been a full five hours since the two parties had left the hollow where the cattle had watered, and since each had taken an opposite bearing, a considerable number of miles would now lie between them.

This fact did not worry Kyler as the bay loped easily on over the grassy plain; he would catch up. For the moment, despite the grim purpose of the ride, he was enjoying the beauty of the warm night. Overhead the stars hung low and bright, and the faintest of breezes fanned his face. Coyotes yapped from the ridges and now and then he heard the muted chirping of birds, disturbed by his passage.

He thought of Wasco, of Bill Denby and the drovers. The old puncher had understood the problem he had faced when confronted by Eli

Hurd and his men. But Denby and the others had been sorely disappointed by the way he had handled the encounter.

Perhaps he should have taken them more into his confidence, but it hadn't occurred to him. A loner all his life, Sam Kyler rarely voiced his intentions, simply went ahead and did what he felt must be done. One thing was certain, the crew would never realize how near to sudden death they were when young Andy decided to take matters into his own hands.

Kyler knew men—and every rider backing Eli Hurd was a gunman and killer. None would have hesitated to open up on the drovers, blast them from their saddles likely before they could even draw their own weapons. Sam Kyler felt good when he thought of that; he had prevented it from happening—at the expense of the crew's respect for him, perhaps—but that didn't matter. They were all alive.

Near midnight he intersected the outlaw's trail. The surrounding country had been growing rougher, and he came upon the welter of hoofprints in a somewhat narrow and ragged canyon.

Halting, he dismounted and studied the tracks. On foot he followed them a short distance, saw that they continued to bear east. He went back onto the bay then rode to the top of a nearby butte for a longer view of the land.

The flat plain had died, he saw, and the country stretching out before him was a shadowy world of arroyos, deep hollows and broken buttes. He stared out across this, wondering why Hurd and his men had not begun to veer south for Dalhart; the thought came to him that the outlaws could be driving the stock to a different railhead.

Such didn't strike him as reasonable. Hurd, in his soaring confidence, would entertain no thoughts of trouble or opposition; he would seek the nearest point where he could dispose of the cattle and collect cash. Such would be Dalhart. Undoubtedly the trail would eventually change its course.

He dropped off the crest, rejoined the tracks. They continued, bearing straight ahead and easily visible in the silvery night. An hour later Kyler became aware of change; the trail was beginning to turn south. He grinned in satisfaction. Eli Hurd was going to Dalhart, as he had figured. And the camp should be nearby. The outlaws would have halted at sundown.

Locating another high butte, he climbed to

the top. From there he swung his gaze to the south, hopeful of detecting the red eye of a campfire. There was nothing—only the pale flats and the dark shadows where the land fell away in the distance.

He allowed his eyes to travel back slowly, thinking perhaps the trail had not made so definite a turn. Abruptly he drew himself up on the saddle. Far ahead a solitary light winked through the night. He studied it closely. It was no campfire but a lamp shining through the window of a house.

Again satisfaction flooded over him. He had stumbled upon the hangout of Hurd and his men. There would be no one else on that desolate, infertile area.

He left the butte and, abandoning the cattle trail, rode in a direct line for the lonely beacon. It was a rough course through steep-sided, sandy floored arroyos, across a broad strip of brakes, but finally he reached the edge of a field, now badly overgrown with brush and weeds. There he pulled to a stop.

Once it had been a homestead—some man's dream of independence; now a rotting rail fence surrounded the small tract, enclosed a sagging frame house and several adjacent sheds and barns, equally deteriorated. A half dozen shade trees, carefully spaced and dead from thirst, stood bare and stark in the night.

The light came from a room at the back of the structure, Kyler saw, and immediately began to work in nearer. Holding the bay to a walk, he approached from a corner of the house, unwilling to risk meeting one of the outlaws who might be outside or close to the door.

He didn't see the horses until he was almost upon them. Halting, he counted them. Nine— and the cattle were not to be seen. It could mean only that part of the outlaws had gone on with the herd while the remainder awaited their return here.

Eli Hurd's party was divided. It was what he had hoped for. Smiling grimly, Sam Kyler continued on for another twenty yards and then, in a thick stand of osage orange, pulled to a stop. Dismounting, he tied the bay securely, and taking his shotgun, proceeded on foot.

Reaching the corner of the house, he paused. He could hear laughter coming from the interior of the structure, along with an occasional oath.

Some of the outlaws were playing cards, he guessed. Likely others were sleeping.

He moved on, planting each step with care. The night was quiet and he realized that any unusual sound—the snapping of a dry branch, the rattle of brush—would carry through the open door and window and be heard by the outlaws.

He gained the window, stopped, peered cautiously around its splintered frame. He was looking into the kitchen of the abandoned house. Five men were gathered around a table engaged in a game of stud poker. A sixth slept in a nearby chair. The remaining three, he assumed, were in one of the adjoining rooms.

A coffeepot sat on the squat, nickel trimmed cook stove placed at one end of the quarters. Several tin cups were stacked beside it. The outlaws, however, confined their interest to a half empty bottle of whiskey before them on the table.

Sam watched silently as a plan built slowly in his mind. He wondered if the back door represented the only exit and entrance to the building. After a moment he doubled back, made his way to the opposite side. There was a front door but apparently never used. Drifted sand had piled up, several inches in depth, against it. Most likely it was barred on the inside.

Satisfied he could expect the men to come and go only by the rear opening, Kyler retraced his steps. Again he halted at the corner, centered his attention this time, however, on the yard. The first of the smaller buildings, a tool shed, stood directly opposite the door at a distance of fifty feet or so. It would serve his purpose ideally.

He spent most of the next hour collecting dry brush and weeds in the field and laying piles against the front and the south side of the old house. When that was done he noted that daylight was not far off.

Taking a match he fired the mounds of brush, and when both were burning briskly, he crossed the yard and took up a position behind the tool shed.

13

THE card game continued.

Tense, Sam Kyler watched smoke rise above the far side of the house, and moments later, along the roof edge of the south wall. An orange tongue of flame appeared, and then a crackling sound broke the hush.

"Somethin's burnin'!" a voice inside the building shouted.

Kyler, crouched behind the shed, kept his eyes on the sagging screen door at the rear of the structure. Abruptly it flung open. Men rushed into the yard, stumbling over one another in their haste.

"It's around the front—"

"Front, hell—the whole works is burnin'!"

Kyler waited patiently. Six of the outlaws were in the open. There were three more to account for before he could make his move. They should make an appearance soon; flames were now shooting above the roof of the tinder dry building and smoke boiled about it in thick, black clouds.

The screen banged again. The missing outlaws trotted into the yard, pulling on clothing as they shouted angry questions at their friends, now collected in a group along the fringe of the flaring firelight.

"How'd it start?"

Kyler, holding the shotgun before him, stepped from behind the tool shed.

"I started it," he said in a voice that reached above the crackling flames.

The outlaws whirled. A man near center yelled: "It's him—Kyler!"

"Keep your hands high!" Sam shouted his warning.

They raised their arms slowly. A heavily built man with a long scar on his face that showed whitely in the glare, said something to the outlaw beside him, then came back to Kyler.

"What d'you want?"

"You," Kyler said in a flat, uncompromising way.

The big outlaw laughed. "Just like that, eh? You come by yourself?"

"Something you'll have to find out," Sam replied.

A moment of silence followed and then

another man said, "What are you figurin' on doin'?"

"Driving you out of the country—one way or another. The ranchers around here have had enough of you."

"So they hired you to do the job."

"All by yourself?"

"I've got help . . ."

Again there was quiet broken only by the roaring flames that had now spread to the roof and were racing through the interior of the house. The heat had grown intense. Sweat glistened on the features of the outlaws but none risked moving.

"So what's the deal?"

"You've got a choice. Throw down your guns and ride out. Stay off the Strip from here on . . . Or else we settle it here and now."

"You ain't much on countin'," the scar-faced man said. "Nine of us to your one."

"This scattergun evens it up," Kyler said. "I'll get four—maybe five—of you the first blast. Rest will be easy—"

"Hell—he's alone!" the big outlaw yelled suddenly, and clawed for his pistol.

Kyler threw himself to one side, fired the off barrel of the shotgun. The scarred outlaw

97

heaved backwards, slammed to the ground as the full charge of shot caught him.

Wheeling fast, he pressed off the other trigger, taking only quick aim at the group. Three of Hurd's men went down. He dropped the empty shotgun, came up with his forty-five.

Guns blasted through the smoke. Bullets thudded into the tool shed, sent up a shower of needle sharp splinters. Kyler felt a slug rip at his sleeve, burn across his arm. He snapped a shot at an outlaw down on one knee and leveling at him. As the man toppled he saw the remaining four racing for their horses. He cut down on the nearest. The outlaw paused in flight, went crashing headlong into the brush.

Sam leaped away from the shed, hoping for another try at the escaping three. The blinding smoke and thick shrubbery concealed them and he could find no target. He hesitated, jerked aside as one of the men lying in the yard threw a final, desperate shot at him, then collapsed.

Wheeling, Kyler dropped to the tool shed as the quick pound of horses rushing away reached him. Grim, he recovered the shotgun, hurriedly replaced the spent shells. He stood there for a long minute, listening, and then walked to where the outlaws lay.

Three were dead. Two others were wounded, but they would live if they could reach a doctor and receive proper treatment.

"Go on—finish the job," one said as Sam looked down at him.

Kyler shook his head. "You'll make it," he replied. "Both of you . . . But if I ever find you in this country again, I sure as hell will finish it. Now, get up. And help your friend there."

Sam stepped back, watched the oulaw stagger to his feet. The second man, hand clamped to one shoulder, managed to get upright unassisted.

"Drop your guns," Kyler said. "Then get on your horses and ride north Dodge isn't far."

"Dalhart's lots closer—"

"You're not going there. Head north. Maybe you'll find a rancher who'll patch you up so's you can reach Dodge."

The outlaws nodded woodenly, turned toward their mounts. Kyler halted them. "I'll say this once more—don't come back. If you do, I'll kill you."

The pair again moved their heads, continued on. Suddenly there was the hammer of running horses coming in fast. Kyler, reacting instantly, hurled himself to the ground. Gunshots smashed through the crackling flames. Sam heard the whine of bullets, saw one of the wounded outlaws sag, go down.

He rolled to his back, gun in hand. He had only the fleeting shadow of one of the riders for a target as the man thundered for the protection of the brush. He triggered the weapon, saw the outlaw fling up his arms and start to fall. And then smoke hid him from view.

Sam remained motionless. The sound of hoofbeats were a fading rhythm, moving south. He got to his feet quickly. The outlaws would have to be stopped before they could overtake Eli Hurd and the rest of his men somewhere between the burning ranchhouse and Dalhart.

He started across the yard at a run. The second of the wounded men, again on his feet after ducking low when his companions opened up, wheeled in fear.

"I'm goin'!" he yelled.

"Be quick about it," Kyler snapped. "And keep remembering what I said about coming back."

"I sure will," the outlaw answered, looking at the bodies in the yard. "You ain't ever layin' eyes on me again!"

Sam, anxious to be in the saddle, waited

impatiently until the wounded man had mounted and pulled away, and then trotted to where the bay was tethered. Climbing onto the big horse, he gave the house a final glance.

It had burned to its rock foundation and the fire was now spreading through the dry weeds and grass, beginning to lick hungrily at the nearest of the smaller structures. Before the day was over the entire homestead would be a charred ruin—never again offering a handy hideout for men outside the law.

Wheeling the bay out of the osage, he rode across the field to the crest of a hill. Pausing there, he looked to the south. There were two riders in the distance.

Immediately he put the bay to a lope. He would have to move fast.

14

THE outlaws hideout was about a day's ride from Dalhart, Kyler estimated, and the herd was likely somewhere near halfway by that hour. It didn't afford him much time in which to overhaul the fleeing riders.

He pushed the bay hard, holding him to the lower ground where he would not be seen by the two men should they be watching their backtrail. He doubted that; after he had downed the third member of their party when they surged in for a final try for him, they had pulled off fast, anxious to put as much ground between themselves and the old ranch as possible.

The bay was not in very good condition. He had received only a few hours rest since leaving Skull Canyon, but thinking it over, Sam concluded the outlaw's mounts were probably in no better shape. They would have been on the move almost continually in the past two days so he could expect them to be far from their best.

He did not realize how accurate that assumption was until an hour later when he broke out of a long, brush studded arroyo onto a flat and saw the outlaws no more than a quarter mile distant—and directly opposite.

They were taking it slow, favoring their horses, allowing them to walk in the hot sun. They saw Kyler ride into the open at the exact moment he located them. Both halted instantly, then driving spurs deep into the flanks of their worn mounts, they wheeled left and rode hard for a ragged bank of buttes a short distance away.

Kyler swung in after them. He crossed a few yards of solid ground, and then was again in the broad, sandy bed of a wash. The bay began to labor in the loose footing and the outlaws. on firmer surface, drew off rapidly.

Just as the bay climbed out of the arroyo, the two men gained the butte and disappeared into the heavy brush skirting its base. Kyler swore softly. Now he would have to dig them out— and that could take hours. He glanced at the sun as the bay raced on. He had hoped to be in Dalhart when Hurd arrived with the cattle. A lengthy delay here would upset that plan.

He drew his pistol, began to veer toward the

right of the brush into which the outlaws had vanished. He covered only a short distance when a rifle cracked spitefully and sand spurted from beneath the bay. Kyler, ducking low, wheeled the big horse sharply toward the shelter of the bluff and leaped from the saddle.

He struck the ground as the rifle barked a second time. The bullet struck a stone, ricocheted noisily off into the warm air. Kyler hurriedly crawled deeper into the tangle of weeds and creosote bushes, halting finally when he came up against the face of the butte.

He paused, listened. The outlaws were on ahead a hundred yards or so, he guessed, and likely now above him hiding in one of the many narrow ravines that gashed the formation. He looked back. There was no break in the steep wall behind him that would enable him to ascend and circle around the pair. He would have to chance it from below.

Gun in hand, he resumed the slow approach, keeping in close to the bluff and making full use of the brush. Every few yards he halted, listened, hopeful of pinpointing the outlaws' exact position. He heard nothing. They were waiting him out, watching for him to expose himself.

Somewhere ahead gravel rattled hollowly. Kyler stopped again, pressed himself tight against the rough, red surface of the butte. A horse stamped wearily—the sound so close that Kyler stiffened. He realized then he was in the same badly overgrown area in which the men had sought cover, that their hastily abandoned horses were only paces away.

The meaning of the spilling gravel came to him; the men were descending, leaving the cut in the butte where they had hidden and taken their shots at him. They were returning, still cautious, for their horses.

"I tell you—I got him . . ."

The hoarse whisper came from Kyler's right and slightly overhead. More displaced shale clattered.

"Was that last shot . . . Seen him go down . . ."

"Maybe . . . But we ain't takin' no chances," another voice said. "I keep rememberin' what that scattergun done to Webb and them others . . . I ain't anxious to buck up again it twice."

The voices had grown louder, the scraping of boots more pronounced.

"Reckon we're the only ones that got away?"

"Wouldn't surprise me none . . ."

"Hurd'll raise holy hell when he finds out—nine of us and only one Kyler . . . What'll we tell him?"

"I'll tell him for you," Sam said and stepped into the center of the draw.

Both outlaws fell back, surprise and fear blanking their faces. The older of the two tripped, fell. A yell burst from his flaring lips.

"Don't shoot!"

"Get up," Kyler said coldly. "Both of you—walk out here—hands high."

The pair moved into the small clearing, the old man complying hastily; the other, a husky redhead, took his time all the while watching Kyler with narrowed eyes.

"Now what?" he asked when they had halted. "You aim to shoot us down?"

"Probably what you've got coming," Sam replied, "but I'm no judge and jury. I'll give you the same choice I offered you before—get out of this country and stay out, or go for your gun."

"I'm for ridin'," the oldster said instantly. "And we won't come back, neither. You got a promise."

"Maybe I can bank on that, and maybe not," Kyler said, "so I'll make you one. I give you my word I'll kill you on sight if I ever run into you again. That clear?"

"Sure is . . ."

"Head north. I don't want you around Dalhart."

"Yes, sir—north," the older outlaw said readily.

Kyler settled his gaze on the redhead. "You're not talking. You agree with the old man?"

The outlaw shrugged. "He's makin' his own deal. I'll do what I figure's best for me."

Sam Kyler felt the tension grow within him. "What's best for you?" he asked softly.

The redhead moved his shoulders again. He was holding the rifle in his left hand. He raised it, broadside, toward Kyler, apparently surrendering the weapon.

"This," he said in a quick, breathless way and threw the long gun straight at Sam. In that same instant his right hand swept down, came up fast with his pistol.

Kyler, warding off the rifle with his left forearm, fired twice in rapid succession. The redhead jerked half around from the impact of the forty-five's bullets, went to his knees. He hung there briefly, then sprawled full length.

Sam Kyler had not removed his eyes from the older man after triggering his weapon. Abruptly his taut shape relented. The oldster had no intention of following his partner's example. He stared at the dead man, then raised his gaze to Sam.

"Was a dang fool—that Red," he muttered. "Anybody'd know better'n try that."

Relieved but still wary, Kyler said: "I take it you got a different idea."

"Yes, sir—sure have. You bein' willin', I'll just climb onto my horse and head north."

Kyler nodded. "That's what I want. Drop your gun and move out."

The outlaw lifted his pistol carefully by the butt, allowed it to fall. Sam stepped forward, kicked it off into the brush.

"This country's not for you," he said. "You got that straight?"

"Yes, sir." The old man hesitated, looked questioningly at Kyler. "It all right if I walk?"

Sam took a step to one side, permitted the outlaw to pass, then fell in behind and followed him to where the horses stood. There could be another rifle. His glance probed the saddle. There had been only one. Silent, he watched the oldster mount.

"Take Red's horse," Kyler said when the outlaw was settled. "No sense leaving him here to starve."

The outlaw nodded, took up the reins of his partner's sorrel. He leaned forward, his features mirroring the relief that filled him.

"Obliged to you for seein' things this way . . ."

Kyler shook his head. "Just don't forget what I told you."

"Ain't no danger of that," the old man said and rode off.

15

SAM KYLER returned to the bay and immediately struck south for Dalhart. He had no hoof-marked trail to follow but he knew in which general direction the settlement lay; the rest of the outlaws, with the herd, should be somewhere in the intervening area.

Two hours later he caught sight of a small dust cloud well off to his right. He angled the tired bay toward it, again taking the precaution of keeping below the horizon as much as possible, and soon was near enough to size up the cattle and drovers.

There were only four riders with the herd; there should be six. Frowning, he considered that. He was certain it was the stolen beef, but he was reluctant to move in closer for a better look. He was still too far from Dalhart to reveal himself.

Puzzled, he cut back east into the choppy hills and circled wide to place himself ahead of the slowly moving herd. Then, in a narrow arroyo choked with rabbitbrush and Apache plume, he waited for the cattle to pass.

He had been right.

The first rider he saw was Shad Collins. Eli Hurd, however, was not among the other three. Apparently he had ridden on ahead with another of his crew to make necessary arrangements for the sale of the cattle.

Kyler heaved a sigh of relief. For a brief time the possibility of there being two small herds on the flats and enroute to the settlement had plagued him. And if he had picked the wrong bunch of steers to follow, his plan for recovering the beef would have been thrown out of kilter.

He permitted the herd to pass, and when it was a safe distance ahead, he broke out of the arroyo and followed slowly. It would have been no great chore to close in on the four riders, overcome them and take possession; but this he had no thought of doing. It was smarter to let them drive the stock to Dalhart than attempt to manage the unruly brutes alone.

The afternoon wore on, hot and dusty. Smoke appeared on the horizon, marking the location of the town. Sam gauged the sun. The herd should reach there an hour or so before dark, he reckoned.

He wondered then if Wasco and the crew had arrived with the main body of the drive, guessed they had unless there had been trouble. He hoped all had gone well. If he could pull off what he had in mind for Eli Hurd all of the beef would reach the loading pens and he and Wasco would have that much of their agreement fulfilled.

He topped out a low rise and the houses and buildings of Dalhart came into view. Almost at once a solitary rider left the scatter of structures and rode out to meet the incoming herd, now a half mile ahead. Kyler again dropped back, swept wide and put himself ahead of the cattle.

At a safe distance he watched the newcomer join Collins and the others, realized that he likely had been dispatched by Hurd to direct the crew when it reached town.

Spurring on, Kyler circled farther east and entered Dalhart from its back side. He had no wish to encounter Eli Hurd just yet. Keeping to the edge of the settlement, he passed behind the shacks and barns that lay along the railroad right-of-way and eventually came to the long string of loading pens and chutes. Most of the pens, he noted were filled to capacity with bawling, heaving cattle.

It required several minutes of persistent searching to locate Hurd. He finally spotted the outlaw in company with a well-dressed man—evidently a cattle buyer—waiting at an empty enclosure at the extreme end of the row. Pulling in behind a small shed Kyler dismounted, anchored the bay and once more settled down to wait.

An hour later, with the sun hovering just above the western horizon, the herd, swathed in a rolling cloud of yellow dust and complaining noisily, appeared at the edge of town and started down the lane leading to the pens.

The outlaw chief and the buyer, a fold of papers in his hand, moved from the shade of the tree under which they had been standing, and crossed to the empty pen. Hurd swung back the gate and the two men stationed themselves at one side. When the first steer entered, the tally began.

Sam Kyler, leaning against the board railing of a fence a few yards away, watched idly. When the last steer was inside and the gate closed, he straightened, and walking quietly, edged in close.

With the securing of the cattle, two of Hurd's riders swung off at once for the center of town, anxious to find a saloon where they could wash away the dust accumulated in their throats. Kyler grinned his satisfaction. That left only three men to side Eli Hurd.

"How many you make it, Jessup?"

It was the outlaw chiefs voice. Kyler paused at the corner of the pen. Hurd said something more but the noise rising from the restless, milling steers drowned his words. Sam moved in closer.

The cattle buyer was working with his pencil. He looked up. "Two hundred seven head . . ."

"Seven more'n I figured," Hurd said, laughing. "Must've picked up some strays."

Jessup smiled, reached into his pocket for a pad of bank drafts. "Now, if you'll turn over your bill of sale so I can jot down the brands—"

"Right here," the outlaw said, taking the folded paper from his vest pocket. "You'll have to make a change in the count. Outside of that everything ought to be jake."

"Know that, Mr. Hurd, but the company insists on things being just so. It all right if I make the draft out to cash?"

"Suits me fine. . . . Now, let's see—you said

114

sixteen fifty a head. . . . And there's two hundred and seven. . . ."

"Comes out to three thousand four hundred and fifteen dollars . . . and fifty cents. Real nice piece of change for a small herd like yours."

The outlaw grinned. "Sure is . . ." He slid a glance at his crew waiting slackly on their saddles.

"Got any more you'd like to sell? Market's top," Jessup said, making notes in his book. "Prime stuff is in demand. . . . Be glad to drop back later on if you've got another bunch you'd like to dispose of."

Hurd plucked at his chin thoughtfully. "Might just take you up on that," he said. "Been my habit to sell just a small bunch every year. That way it sort of keeps the main herd from runnin' down. . . ."

One of the riders laughed. The outlaw chief seemed not to hear. "But what you're sayin' makes sense. Could be I might scare up a couple hundred more. . . ."

"Fine, fine. Just leave word at the bank. They'll get in touch with me," Jessup said, snapping his book shut. "Well, guess that takes care of everything. Here's your draft. . . ."

Eli Hurd raised his arm, reached for the slip of paper.

"I'll take that," Sam Kyler said from the shadows, and drew back the twin hammers of his shotgun.

16

AT the dry, over-loud clack of the weapon being cocked the outlaws froze. Jessup stared.

"Stand easy," Kyler said in a low voice. "Nobody moves—nobody gets hurt."

"Who the hell are you?" Hurd demanded angrily.

"The man you just made a deal for," Sam replied quietly.

He moved to the side of Jessup, plucked the draft from the man's fingers and tucked it into his shirt pocket. Backing off, he circled around until he faced the men.

Eli Hurd stiffened. "Kyler!" he muttered under his breath.

Sam placed his attention on Jessup. "You bought yourself some rustled cattle, mister. Were part of a big herd I was driving in."

"Stolen!" Jessup said in a strangled voice. "There was a bill of sale—"

"He got it at gunpoint. . . ."

Jessup frowned, looked questioningly at the

outlaw chief. Hurd's expression did not change. He continued to glare at Kyler. The rider next to Collins shifted. Shad threw him a hurried glance.

"Forget it, Bud . . . He'll cut you in two with that damned scatter gun."

"He's no cattleman," Kyler continued. "He's nothing but an outlaw—a rustler. Every cow he ever sold you was pirated from somebody's herd."

"First time I ever bought from him," Jessup said defensively. He turned to Hurd. "This all true?"

"Hell no—it ain't true!" the outlaw said boldly. "If you got the time, I can take you to my place. North of here, about a day's ride—"

"I burned it to the ground," Kyler drawled. "Your boys have pulled out—ones that aren't dead."

Hurd's mouth snapped shut. Sweat stood out on his forehead in large beads. "You trailed my boys—"

"Right. Had a little talk with them. Those that were reasonable moved on—said they'd not be back."

"And the others?"

"Buzzard bait."

Hurd shook his head in disbelief. "I ain't swallowin' none of that," he said, and then as his surprise at seeing Sam Kyler faded and a measure of his effrontery returned, he added, "He's feedin' you a lot of guff, Jessup. Cattle don't belong to him. He's just a damn drifter tryin' to cash in on a good thing."

The buyer mopped his flushed face, looked at Sam. "That true? You don't own the stock?"

"Told you I was driving them through. Belong to the cattlemen on the Strip. You'll find the rest of the herd in the pens along here somewhere. Be easy enough to check the brands."

"Well—I don't know," Jessup said hesitantly. "Never came up against anything like this before."

"You're in the clear," Kyler said. "Money will go to the right men now . . . Be obliged to you if you'll go get the marshal."

"The marshal!" Eli Hurd shouted. "What for? He's got no call to go buttin' into this."

"Maybe he has. Rustling took place outside his territory—I know that. But the deal you were trying to pull happened right here in his town. I figure that makes it his business." Kyler paused, drifted the muzzle of the shotgun

119

suggestively over Hurd and his riders. "Drop your hardware. Do it slow."

Shad Collins was the first to obey. He lifted his weapon with his left hand, allowed it to fall into the loose dust. The outlaw beside him, Bud, followed suit. The tall rider standing near Hurd simply stared.

"How about it?" Kyler pressed quietly.

The man hesitated a moment longer, then shrugged, reached for his pistol.

"The hell with it!" Hurd shouted abruptly and lunged against Jessup.

Kyler leaped back, tried to get out of the way of the reeling cattle buyer. He was too slow. Jessup slammed into him and they both went down. He was aware of Hurd's voice yelling something, of the quick hammer of horses pulling away as Shad Collins and Bud made a run for it.

He jerked clear of Jessup, got to his feet. Instantly a gunshot smashed through the darkness and a bullet thudded into a cross board of the cattle pen behind him. He whirled, caught a glimpse of the tall outlaw, let him have the left barrel of the shotgun. The rider staggered back, fell.

Again Kyler heard the pound of running

horses. He turned, had a glimpse of Bud and Collins, both with rifles—and the two missing members of Hurd's crew. He realized what had taken place; Shad and Bud, fleeing, had immediately run into the other outlaws as they were returning from town. They had joined forces and were coming to Eli Hurd's aid.

Sam fired at the two nearest. He saw both go off their saddles as the load of buckshot ripped into them. He dropped the shotgun, drew his revolver and spun. He snapped a shot at the third rider—Shad Collins—missed.

From the corner of his eye he saw Hurd running hard for the far end of the cattle pen. Sam leveled on him, checked, and ducked away as a gun roared close by and a bullet slapped into the wood behind him. He looked up, saw Shad and Bud coming in again.

He triggered a shot at Bud, saw him wilt and cut away, almost colliding with Collins. He tried once more, this time for Shad, again missed. Through the coiling smoke he saw them both wheel sharp and disappear into the darkness beyond the brush. Sam drew in close to the cattle pen, listening hard. Jessup was a few feet away, lying flat on the ground trying desperately to keep out of the line of fire.

"My God—I never saw such a—"

"Shut up!" Kyler hissed.

He was uncertain as to the intentions of Bud and Shad Collins. They could be moving in again. He heard hoofbeats, relaxed slightly. They were heading into town. They'd had enough. He looked at the cattle buyer.

"Stay put . . . And you won't get hurt."

Crouching low, Kyler began to move along the side of the pen. The shadows were black in that area and he could determine very little distinctly, but he was between Eli Hurd and his horse and he was sure the outlaw was still there.

Off toward town he could hear shouting. The splatter of gunshots had attracted attention. Soon a crowd would gather—a crowd that would include not only the curious but the representatives of the law as well. Earlier he would have welcomed the town marshal's presence—but now it was different. It would be difficult to make the lawman understand his position—and the shootout. Best thing to do was find Hurd quickly, settle with him—and move on.

He reached the end of the pens. Still hunkered, he stopped, searched the dark pools beyond for the outlaw. He could see no sign of the man. Hurd would not have gone far; at that very moment he would be nearby in hiding, waiting for Kyler to step into the open and provide him with an easy mark.

Considering that briefly, Sam retreated a few steps, turned and climbed over the top rail of the pen and dropped into the midst of the cattle. Shoving his way through the restless animals, he crossed to the opposite side. Removing his hat, he peered over the top board.

He saw Eli Hurd.

The outlaw was squatting behind a stump only paces away, his face turned toward the corner of the pen. He had been waiting just as Sam had anticipated.

Kyler drew himself upright. "Last chance, Eli . . . Throw down your—"

Before he could finish the outlaw leader whirled and fired. The bullet smashed into the dry timber in front of Kyler, spewed dust and stinging splinters. Sam got off two quick shots. The outlaw staggered to his feet, went back to his knees. He hung there for several moments struggling to again lift his gun, and then fell forward.

Kyler vaulted the fence, threw a hurried

glance at the approaching crowd. It was not far away. Wheeling, he ran the width of the pen, rounded the corner and legged it to where Jessup lay.

Scooping up the shotgun, he paused beside the cattle buyer.

"When the marshal gets here—see that you tell the story straight," he said in a hard voice.

Jessup scrambled to his feet. He nodded vigorously. "I will . . . I sure will."

Turning, Sam Kyler trotted to where the bay waited.

17

KYLER hurried back along the route he had previously followed, keeping to the darkness at the rear of the buildings. He could hear shouting near the cattle pens, realized the crowd had reached that point and was having its look at what had happened there. He would be pressed for time, he knew; but with a little luck he should be able to find the bank and transact his business and then join Wasco and the crew at the Longhorn Saloon before Dalhart's lawman got a search underway.

He came finally to what he judged to be the center of town and halted. Leaving the bay behind a small shed, he made his way along a passage that ran between two of the buildings and came out onto the main street.

He paused again, faced the blast of sound running through the clouds of spinning dust. Dalhart was bulging at the seams with drovers, just paid-off and all endeavoring to spend their earnings in a single night. He studied the throng surging up and down the street,

125

concluded he would likely go unnoticed. He had visited the town only once before, and except for Shad Collins and Bud and perhaps someone he might accidently bump into, he was not known.

He moved to the edge of the walk, ran his glance along the store-fronts in search of the bank. He had no difficulty in locating the Longhorn Saloon—and wished then he had named a less prominent place for the meeting with Wasco and the crew. It was ablaze with light and there was a continual flow in and out of its batwing doors.

The Cattleman's Trust, he saw then, was immediately to his right. Stepping into the loose dust, Kyler shouldered his way to the structure. It was open, as were all business houses, despite the fact that the day was over; Dalhart merchants were making the most of their opportunities. Reaching the bank, he crossed the board walk and entered.

Two armed men sitting on opposite sides of the narrow room rose to their feet, eyed him suspiciously. Ignoring them, Kyler stepped up to the one occupied cage. He dug Jessup's draft from his pocket, shoved it under the grillwork.

"Want this cashed."

The teller, an elderly individual with steel-rimmed spectacles, nodded, studied the face of the order. "Your name?"

"Sam Kyler."

The banker shook his head. "Guess it doesn't make any difference . . . Jessup's always making these things out to cash. How do you want it?"

"Big bills," Sam replied and removed his money belt and laid it on the shelf before him.

He waited until the ranchers' money had been counted then pushed it aside and emptied the pockets of the belt. He was short a hundred dollars or so of Arch Clayborn's thousand and he considered claiming an advance from what was owed him by the Strip ranchers. There should be no objection. The worst of the trip was over; all that remained was the return, and if he followed Tolliver's suggestion there would be no danger of losing the ranchers' cash to outlaws.

But somehow it didn't seem right to him. He handed the bills to the teller. "Like to have a draft for that. Make it out to Arch Clayborn. Burnt Springs, Texas."

The banker counted the currency and loose silver, reached for a blank check. "Even nine hundred—or you want to include the odd amount, too?"

"Make it nine hundred," Kyler replied.

It wouldn't matter; he intended to send Clayborn the difference as soon as he was paid. He stuffed the ranchers' money into his belt, fastened it around his waist. Picking up the cash returned to him by the teller, he thrust it into his pocket.

"Like to borrow an envelope and sheet of paper," he said. "Stamp, too, if you've got one."

The banker paused, produced the required items. "How about a pen and some ink?" he said, his tone faintly sarcastic.

Kyler grinned. "Pencil will do," he said and obtained one from his own pocket.

He addressed the envelope to Clayborn, then wrote a short note explaining what had happened. He ended the letter with a promise to mail the missing one hundred dollars within a few days. By the time he had finished the banker was ready.

"Be a dollar service charge," he said handing over the draft.

Sam paid off, enclosed the draft with the letter and sealed them inside the envelope.

Affixing the stamp, he looked questioningly at the banker.

"Leave it with me," the man said tiredly. "I'll see it gets posted."

"Obliged," Kyler said and passing the letter to him, returned to the street.

He halted in the darkness just outside the door, stared off into the noisy night. Weariness and hunger were beginning to drag at him but he knew it was unsafe to remain in Dalhart. Better to look up Wasco and the others, head out and then when they were a reasonable distance from the town, stop for the night. Wheeling, he started down the walk for the Longhorn—suddenly drew up.

Two men had emerged from the saloon next to the bank. One was Jessup, the other was a tall, wide-shouldered man wearing a star. Sam flattened himself against the wall.

"Maybe he was in the right," the marshal was saying. "But nobody rides into my town, shoots up a half dozen men and rides out scot-free . . . Can't afford to let a thing like that happen."

"They were outlaws, Marshal. Admitted it."

"Still men—and far as this Kyler goes, he ain't no better. Got a wanted dodger in my

129

office for him right now. Stole a thousand dollars from some Texas rancher." The lawman paused. "Sure you got no idea where he was headed?"

"Don't recall him mentioning it. Just got on his horse and rode off. Could be putting up here for the night."

"Doubt that. Kyler's been around. He knows I'll be looking for him. You say he was working for the ranchers over on the Strip?"

"What he claimed."

"He'll be goin' back there then. Be wanting to collect his pay."

"You aim to go after him, Gates?"

"What else? He'll have to answer to that robbery charge—and I sure can't let him get by with what he done here . . . If I did, I'd have every lousy guntoter this side of the Missouri thinking he could do the same."

"But that's unclaimed territory. There's no law—"

"It'll have some when I get there," the marshal said grimly and started to turn. "Let's go take a look at that dodger. Want to be sure it's the same man."

Kyler watched them move off into the crowd. Arch Clayborn had filed charges, as he had feared the rancher would. He gave that bitter thought for a moment, then shrugged. He couldn't blame Clayborn; it did look like robbery. But it would all be cleared up when the rancher received his draft.

Meanwhile it would be smart to keep out of the lawman's way, as he had planned. He could talk better in Jericho. For all Gates' strong words he could do nothing once he was in the Strip. Once there he could explain the Clayborn matter, persuade him to wait, give Arch time to withdraw the charges.

As to the lawman's other complaint, he could understand his position. Any kind of a shootout was bad for a town, and while he had not fired the first bullet, there was no denying he had sought out Eli Hurd and his men for the express purpose of settling with them. He could explain that too, back in Jericho—and he would have the Strip ranchers to stand behind him.

Kyler moved away from the wall, looked down the street. Jessup and Gates had disappeared. The next thing was to meet Wasco and the crew, pull out. He stepped off the board walk into the loose dust, slanted toward the Longhorn.

"Kyler!"

131

At the sound of Shad Collins' voice, Sam dipped and wheeled from instinct. He saw the outlaw, flanked by Bud, standing in the entrance to the building adjoining the saloon. In the next instant he looked into the orange flash of Shad's pistol, felt the shock of a bullet as it tore through the fleshy part of his leg. And then he was triggering his own weapon.

Shad Collins fired a second time but from pure spasmodic reflex. The slug splintered the door behind him. Bud had leaped back out of harm's way, his good arm raised above his head. A bandage showed whitely on the other.

"I ain't part of this!" he yelled.

Kyler's rigidity broke. His gun lowered. Men were shouting in the street, surging toward him. He became aware of the pain in his leg and the wry thought that he had gone through two shootouts without serious injury, only to take a bullet there on Dalhart's crowded street as he faced one man, passed through his mind.

Recognition of danger suddenly pushed all else aside. Gates would be coming with the crowd. Limping badly, he finished his crossing and ducked into the passageway that ran alongside the Longhorn.

Reaching the corner of the bulky structure,

he turned, saw a short staircase leading up to a landing. Ignoring the pain in his leg, he climbed the steps, pushed open the door. He was in a narrow hallway at the end of which a second door faced him. He moved hurriedly to it, drew it back. A wave of noise, light, smoke and confusion struck him head on. He had entered the Longhorn from the rear.

The place was packed. Several men standing at the bar to his left glanced up at his abrupt appearance, then looked away disinterestedly. Evidently the back door was in common usage.

Sam, keeping close to the end of the counter in an effort to hide his wounded leg from the curious, worked toward the front. He saw Wasco at the same moment the old puncher recognized him. Sam halted, watched his friend lean across the table where he was sitting and tap Bill Denby on the arm. Together the two men rose and made their way through the crowd to Kyler.

"Sure glad to see you!" Wasco exclaimed, then drew back. "You been shot up!"

Kyler shook his head. "No time to explain now. Got to get out of town—"

Denby said, "The law?"

Sam nodded. "Out front now—looking for

133

me. Get the boys together and head north. I'll meet you down the trail four or five miles."

"Ought to get that leg fixed first—" the rancher said.

"No time. Going to be a chore getting to my horse."

"Don't worry about the law," Wasco said, his weathered face breaking into a grin. "Me and the boys'll keep him busy for a spell while you're gettin' started. You need anythin'?"

"Nothing—except to get out of Dalhart," Kyler said and turned for the door.

"We'll sure guarantee that," Wasco promised. "See you down the line."

"One thing more," Denby called, and as Kyler hesitated, he added, "How about the stock—you get it back?"

Sam patted the money belt under his shirt. "Got the money right here."

The rancher smiled. "And Eli Hurd?"

"Taken care of," Kyler replied and moved on.

18

KYLER waited in the darkness at the rear of the Longhorn. His leg throbbed relentlessly and a dampness along his knee warned him that the wound was bleeding freely. Jerking the bandanna from around his neck he impatiently ripped it into two strips, tied them together and improvised a bandage. Placing it over the wound, he pulled it tight. Breathing heavily from his efforts, he leaned back against the building. That was all he could do for the injury for the present.

A wild burst of yelling, punctuated by a solitary gunshot, rose above the general hubbub of confusion in the street fronting the saloon. Kyler grinned tautly. Wasco and the drovers were creating their diversion. He delayed another few moments, allowing ample time for the crowd to collect, then crossed the open passageway and entered the shadows on the opposite side.

He could hear men running, shouting questions, but the passageway had offered only a

135

fleeting glimpse of the street, and he could just guess at what was taking place; a fight, a staged free-for-all, most likely.

Kyler kept to the rear of the buildings until he was some distance below the Longhorn, and then cut back to the sidewalk. He found he was a hundred yards or so from the large crowd gathered in the glaring lights of the saloon. There were still a few persons scattered along the way, unattracted by the excitement, and he paused to give them thorough scrutiny. Town Marshal Gates was not one of them and Kyler immediately crossed over, walking leisurely so as to not draw undue attention.

He gained the opposite side of the street, stepped into the nearest passageway, and broke into a slow, painful jog. He came out below the shed where he had tied the bay, veered left through a jumble of old casks, packing boxes and other trash.

Almost upon the shed, he pulled up short. Two men, standing beside the bay, wheeled at his sudden appearance. Alarm rocked through Kyler—and then died. Neither of the pair was Gates.

The taller of the two faced Sam. He jerked a thumb at the big horse. "Yours?"

Sam nodded, moved in closer. "Figured I ought to leave him back here," he said, giving the reins a yank to release the knot. "Hell of a commotion out there on the street."

The man shrugged. "On my property. Was about to lead him off to the pound." He shifted his glance, eyed the horse critically. "Looks mighty beat. Expect he could use a good feed."

"He'll get it," Kyler said and swung to the saddle.

The second of the two came up sharply. "Say —you been shot?"

"Only a scratch," Sam replied and started to pull away.

"Scratch, hell—that's a bullet hole!" The man paused, stared. "By God—you're the fellow the marshal's lookin' for!" he said in a breathless voice.

Kyler hauled in, came half around. His jaw was set. "Take your time telling him about it," he said in a slow, quiet way. "Don't want trouble with you . . ."

The two men froze. Kyler favored them with a curt nod, and moved on.

Dismissing them from his mind, Sam rode due south for the full length of the town, then cut right. When he crossed the road leading up to Dalhart's main street, the racket in front of the Longhorn and elsewhere in the settlement was only a faint churning sound beneath a pale glare.

He continued his westward course until the town lay well behind him, and then again veered right. A short time later he reached the trail that led, eventually, to Jericho and points on north, and swung onto it.

His leg was paining considerably and he held the bay to a slow lope, hopeful of minimizing the discomfort, but it helped little. Realizing, finally, that nothing would ease the leg except rest, he clamped his teeth shut and rode on.

He pulled off the trail short of the distance he had stipulated. A large outcropping of rock, well covered with brush and purple tassled grass offered an inviting place to await Wasco and the crew, and he halted gratefully in the shallow coulee and dismounted.

Moving stiffly, he sat down and sank back against a ledge of sandstone as the bay began to graze eagerly. He made a brief examination of his wound. There was nothing more he could do for it until the crew arrived, which should be soon. Wasco would lose no time in pulling out of Dalhart.

His thoughts turned to Gates, the lawman. He would be passing that way, too, if he followed through with his intentions. But it was doubtful if he would begin the journey to Jericho before morning. And by then Sam Kyler expected to be well on his way. He had little to worry about insofar as the marshal was concerned, he decided.

A half hour later the sound of running horses reached him. He pulled himself erect, limped to the outermost point of the rocky formation and waited. He must first be certain it was the crew before showing himself; if so, he would have to act quickly and stop them. They were expecting to meet him farther on.

He recognized Wasco well before the riders drew abreast and caught the old puncher's attention by waving his hat. Immediately the crew left the trail and moments later all were gathered in the coulee.

"Got here fast as we could," Wasco said, grinning broadly. "Marshal was for juggin' the bunch of us for startin' the ruckus, but we sort've talked him out of it."

"Cost us twenty dollars—disturbin' the peace," Bill Denby said. "You have any trouble leavin'?"

Kyler shook his head. Wasco looked at him with critical eyes.

"How's that there leg?"

"Could use some attention. Anybody got a bottle of whiskey?"

"Me—I have," one of the men said.

"Bring it," Wasco directed before Kyler could speak. He squatted down and began to examine the wound. "I'll do the doctorin'. Rest of you get a fire goin'—boil up some coffee. And dig out the grub." He looked up at Sam. "When'd you eat last?"

Kyler shook his head. "Can't remember."

"Just what I figured," the old puncher mumbled. "Shake your tails there, boys. This man ain't dyin' from a gunshot, he's dyin' from a empty belly . . ."

An hour later Sam Kyler was feeling much better. His hunger had vanished and Wasco had done a good job on the leg, first cleaning it with hot water, then cauterizing with the fiery liquor, after which he wrapped it with bandages made from a shirt. He was ready to move on but the old puncher would not hear of it.

"We're stayin' put—leastwise until daylight. You're in for a devil of a mean ride even then."

"Have to be gone by then," Kyler said, and explained about Gates.

Wasco relented. "All right, then, we'll pull out a couple hours afore sunup. Ought to give us a good lead."

"Not so much that," Kyler said. "We'll be taking a different trail. Point is I want to be in Jericho when he gets there."

Bill Denby looked up from the fire. His features showed surprise. "You ain't goin' back with us?"

"Not taking any chances on losing the money," Kyler said. "Wasco and I'll be taking the road west of here, along the bluffs. You and the crew will go the usual way."

The rancher frowned. Wasco slapped his hands together. "By dang—I see what you're doin'! If them owlhoots aim to jump us, they'll be waitin' somewheres along the trail the boys always use. You're aimin' to decoy them while you and me's hightailin' it down another road!"

"That's the general idea," Sam said. He put his attention on Denby. "Up to you to make it look good. Keep the crew together and when they move in on you, don't put up a fight. No need of anybody getting hurt."

"What happens when they don't find the

141

money on us? They're goin' to be real peeved and start askin' a lot of questions."

"Tell them. By then Wasco and I will be too far ahead for them to catch up."

Denby reached for the coffeepot. "Why don't I just say we left the money in the bank at Dalhart. That'd end it for sure."

"Suit yourself. Just don't get anybody hurt."

Denby leaned forward, squinted. "Reckon this is as good a time as any to say this, Kyler. Had some wrong thoughts about you when this thing started. I'm takin' them back now."

"Forget it," Sam replied. "Expect I could have made it easier for everybody if I'd done a little talking."

Andy, the young puncher who had almost precipitated serious trouble at Rifle Creek, nodded vigorously. "Same goes for me, Mr. Kyler. I'm mighty sorry." He brushed his hat to one side. "That hoedown you had at the cattle chutes sure must've been a humdinger! Folks in town was really talkin' about it. That the way you handled the rest of them outlaws?"

"They won't be around." Sam said quietly, and turned again to Denby. "Where've you got the money?"

"My saddlebags. Couldn't get it in a belt."

"Switch it to mine. Buckle it in tight." He paused, looked around. "Where's the chuck wagon?"

One of the drovers laughed. "Still in Dalhart, I expect. Ranchers' wives give old Turkey a list long as your arm for stuff to get for them. Bet he ain't home for a week."

"You want some grub to take along?" Denby asked. "We brought plenty with us."

Kyler shook his head. "We can hold out until we reach Jericho. With all that cash riding with us, we won't take time to eat."

19

DAYLIGHT caught Sam Kyler and Wasco well on the return to Jericho. They struck the line of low, red faced bluffs, as Tolliver had said, five miles or so west of the main trail, and now were bearing due north. So far the route had not been difficult, but looking ahead Sam could see why it was not practical for a cattle drive.

There was little forage. The ground was sandy, produced nothing other than common soaptree yucca, prickly-pear and snakeweed. Here and there a gaunt cholla reached its barbed fingers toward the sun, and in the deeper arroyos and washes, Apache plume and creosote bush formed scraggly barriers against the occasional torrents of water following the infrequent rainstorms.

"When you figure we'll hit town?" Wasco asked as they moved slowly on under the hot sun.

Kyler shifted himself to one side in an effort

to ease the monotonous pain that claimed his leg. "About midnight—if we keep at it."

The old puncher spat. "Which we sure can't. Horses won't last—and you won't neither. That there leg of your'n is givin' you fits right now."

Sam made no reply. The wound throbbed incessantly, making it impossible to ride in any degree of comfort. But he refused to halt; with almost fifty thousand dollars in their possession, he was anxious to reach Jericho and relieve himself of the responsibility as soon as possible. Anger brushed through him.

"Ranchers are damned fools for not having a bank to deal with," he said irritably. "Carting this much money around is plain loco!"

"Expect they'd sure do it, has they the chance."

"They did. Let the outlaws buffalo them out of it."

Wasco sighed. "Now, you got a good look at them people. Ain't nothin' but ranchers— farmhands turned cowpokes. Couldn't none of them buck the likes of Eli Hurd and his bunch . . ."

"Could if they'd get together . . ." Kyler snapped.

Wasco gave his partner a close look. Sweat

145

was standing out on Kyler's face in broad, shining patches, and his lips were pulled taut from pain. The old rider shifted on his saddle.

"Smidgin' of shade up there ahead," he said pointing at a clump of brush clinging to the rim of a deep gouge in the arroyo. "What say we pull up and rest a spell? Old bones of mine are mighty achy."

Kyler swung his glance to Wasco, grinned knowingly. "All right—but you're not fooling me. And quit coddling me . . . I'll make it."

"Coddlin'—hell! Just plain good sense I'm usin'. You keep on way you're doin'—and we never will get to Jericho!"

They halted for a half hour, then moved on, inaugurating a procedure followed thereafter throughout the day, of riding and resting periodically. It irked Sam Kyler but he was forced to admit that Wasco was right; it was far wiser to arrive in Jericho late than not at all.

Near the end of the afternoon they reached wilder country. The buttes lifted higher, forming canyons in some places, and the trail narrowed until it was little more than an indefinite path wandering along the base of steep walls and through brush filled defiles.

"Slow goin'," Wasco remarked, casting a

glance at the lowering sun. "We won't be makin' town soon if we have much of this."

Kyler, holding himself off the saddle by locking his hands on the horn and cantle, looked back. The old puncher was only a few strides behind.

"Can't be much farther. According to Bill Denby the bluffs end—"

The sudden blast of a gun almost under the bay drowned Sam Kyler's words. The big horse shied violently, reared. Another pistol roared and Kyler heard Wasco yell. The thought *hold-up*, raced through his mind, but he could see no one—nor could he get at his weapon. The bay was plunging recklessly about in the brush, frantic with fear, trying to find stable footing so he could run.

Again guns crackled. Hanging to the reins with one hand, the saddle horn with the other, Kyler ducked as he felt the breath of a bullet. In the same instant the bay started down. Kyler kicked free of the stirrups, jumped. He came down solidly on his injured leg. It gave and he pitched forward into a shelf of rock. He was briefly aware of more gunshots, and then pain and darkness engulfed him as his head smashed against the rough surface of the shelf.

It was full dark when Sam Kyler regained consciousness. He lay quiet, some inner instinct holding him motionless until he was certain all danger had passed.

Hearing nothing, he stirred, endeavored to sit up. He lay face down at the base of the bluff, head lower than his feet. The bay had pitched him into a small, but deep, wash.

Pain roared through him when he heaved himself around. Ignoring that, and the dull throbbing in his head, he got shakily to his feet, stared vacantly into the silence. It was full dark and he could see very little. His foggy mind began to function normally again, and with that came realization. It had been an ambush—a robbery!

Wasco!

He stiffened. Where was he—what had happened to him? Moving as hurriedly as possible, Sam climbed up onto the trail, started back along its uneven course. A dozen paces on and he saw the old puncher stretched full length on the sand, both arms outflung. Kyler, grim and wincing from pain, hobbled to his side and knelt down. He rolled the man to his back, peered into his face. Blood smeared the side of his head, had hardened into a crust.

"Wasco!" Kyler said in a hard, urgent way, shaking him gently. "Wasco!"

The puncher stirred weakly, relapsed into stillness. Water. That would bring him around. The canteens were on their saddles. Kyler rose, looked up the narrow canyon, turned about, probed the area below. There was no sign of the two horses.

Swearing softly, he dropped back to Wasco's side, again shook him. The old man opened his eyes, stared wonderingly into Kyler's face. After a few moments he sat up, rubbed at his head gingerly.

"Somethin' sure give me a hell of a wallop," he muttered thickly.

Kyler sank back onto the sand in relief. "Bullet grazed you."

Wasco nodded. "Mite close . . . How 'bout you?"

"Horse threw me, hit my head on some rocks. Guess that's all that saved my hide. Whoever it was figured us both dead."

The old puncher stared off into the shadows. "Got the money, too, I reckon."

"And the horses . . ."

"The stinkin' varmints—leavin' a man afoot in country like this—"

149

"Figured we wouldn't need them."

"Could've just wandered off . . ."

"Maybe . . ."

Sam Kyler's reply was without conscious effort. He was thinking about the hold-up—and its meaning.

"Was a mighty neat ambush," Wasco said. "What's botherin' me is how'd they know we was comin' this way? Figured it was all a big secret."

Kyler said, "Bothers me, too. Only one other man knew about it—the same man who suggested we take it."

Wasco leaned forward, frowned "Who?"

"Tolliver . . ."

The puncher rocked back in surprise. "The big muckity-muck of the ranchers?"

Sam nodded. "Pulled me off to one side before we left. Told me about this trail. Said it would be a good way to fool the outlaws."

Wasco groaned. "And we walked smack dab into his trap, like a bunch of sheep." After a moment he shook his head. "Sure hard to believe. Figured that Tolliver for a square shooter."

"Had him wrong, too. Guess it worked out just the way he planned. His bunch caught us cold, got the money and rode off leaving us for dead. When we don't show up the ranchers will figure we kept going with the money—or the outlaws got us . . . Nobody'll ever think Tolliver was in on it."

Kyler angrily pulled himself upright. Wasco followed, slightly unsteady.

"Only thing wrong with his figuring," Sam said, "is that we're not dead. We're going to fool him—we're making it to Jericho, somehow."

"On that leg you ain't goin' nowhere far."

"I can manage it. Help me find a stick—a cane. Be slow but I—"

"Just maybe you won't have to try," Wasco cut in, his head cocked to one side. "If I ain't mistook, I heard a horse . . ."

Hope lifted within Sam Kyler. "You sure?"

"Sounded like a shoe clickin' against a rock," the old puncher said. "Stay put whilst I have a look."

Wasco shambled off down the trail. Kyler settled back, shoulders to the wall of the butte. Like the old man, he was finding it hard to believe Tom Tolliver was behind the ambush and robbery, but the facts were indisputable. It could be no one else. . . .

"Found 'em!"

Wasco's voice echoed through the darkness in the narrow slash. Kyler rose to his feet. He could hear the puncher's boots crunching on the sand, the dull thud of hooves as he led their mounts back.

"Was dôwn there grazin', happy as you please."

Relief coursed through Sam Kyler—relief and satisfaction, as he watched Wasco approach. Tom Tolliver was in for one hell of a surprise. . . .

20

THEY reached Jericho shortly after noon. Halting at the end of the street, Sam Kyler threw his glance along its dusty length. There were horses standing at the Fargo's rack—along with Shinn Thompson's buggy. More waited in front of the Palace and Rufe Eggert's place.

"Crew beat us home," Wasco commented idly. "That there's Denby's buckskin next to Thompson's rig. . . . You figure Tolliver'll still be hangin' around?"

"He'll be here," Kyler replied. "He'll be waiting at the hotel with others, making it look good."

"How you aimin' to handle things?"

Kyler shrugged. "Only way I know how. Walk right in and tell them what happened. Then throw the loop on Tolliver."

Wasco nodded approval. "Just what ought to be done. . . ."

Sam touched the tired bay with his spurs, and they moved into the street and pointed for the Fargo's hitchrack. He saw several of the merchants appear in the doorways of their establishment—one of them Marcia Ashwick—stare and then smile quickly when they recognized him. They, too, had a surprise coming, he thought; only it would not be a pleasant one.

As he and Wasco halted at the rail, there was sudden commotion in the hotel's entrance. Before they could dismount a dozen ranchers and townsmen rushed out onto the porch—Tolliver among them. The big rancher, beaming, pushed forward, hand outstretched.

"Mighty happy to see you two!" he shouted. "Denby's been tellin' how you done things—got the cattle through and took care of Hurd and his bunch . . . Was a great job!"

Kyler, favoring his injured leg, came off the saddle and leaned heavily against the bay. His cold glance touched the rancher, reached beyond him. On the porch he could see Shinn Thompson, Pritchard, Dave Simon, Weil, Pete Clark—several more he had not met. He brought his attention back to Tolliver. The man was covering up well.

"Was a great job *you* done," he said finally in a slow, distinct voice. "Plan of yours worked good."

Tolliver frowned. The men standing on the porch fell silent, struck by Kyler's quiet tone.

"Meanin' what?" the rancher asked.

Kyler pulled open his shirt. Removing the money belt he tossed it to Tolliver. "Here's the rest of the cash. Your boys overlooked it when they ambushed us in the brakes. . . ."

Tolliver caught the belt. His jaw sagged. "What the hell you talkin' about . . . Ambush —my boys—"

"You know what I'm talking about," Kyler snarled, coming around. He limped forward leaned against the rack and faced the men on the porch. "We got held-up on the trail. Outlaws took your money, left us for dead."

A mutter of surprised comment ran through the crowd. Shinn Thompson elbowed his way to the edge of the gallery.

"You tellin' us the cattle money's been lost again?"

"I am . . . Hit us in the rough country southwest of here . . . Along the buttes." Kyler's hand lowered, came to rest on the butt of his pistol. "Only man to know we were coming that trail was Tolliver . . . Better ask him where your money is."

"Tolliver!" Thompson shouted in amazement. "You mean he—"

The rancher's mouth was still agape. He stared at Kyler, then to the men on the porch. "That's crazy," he cried in a strangled voice. "I—I never—"

His jaw clamped shut immediately. He stepped in close to Kyler. "You're wrong," he said in a quick way, "dead wrong—but I see your thinkin' . . . Maybe I got the answers."

"Sure goin' to take some good ones," Wasco said dryly.

The muttering on the gallery had risen. Tolliver raised his hand. His face was serious. "Think I know what this is all about . . . Go on back in the hotel and wait. All I want's fifteen minutes—"

"So's you can get out of town?" a voice asked.

"You know me better'n that!" the rancher snapped angrily. He wheeled to Kyler. "Sure —I told you about that back trail—but it wasn't my idea."

"Then who—"

"Rufe Eggert. He mentioned it to me. And earlier this mornin' them six hardcases you tangled with over at Marcy Ashwick's rode in

156

from that direction. They're at Rufe's now. Got a hunch they know plenty about it."

Kyler turned, pulled the shotgun from its boot. He was feeling better. He had found it difficult to believe Tom Tolliver would be involved in the crime, and it was good to realize he had been right.

"Let's pay Eggert a call," he said.

Tolliver threw the money belt he was holding to Pritchard, said, "Keep everybody inside, Al. Could be real trouble," and headed off down the street with Kyler and Wasco.

A distance short of the saloon Sam halted. "His place got a back door?"

Tolliver, face grim, nodded. "Sure has. Around this way. . . ."

He led them down the side of the harness shop, cut right and paused at the rear of a low roofed building. Pointing to a closed door, he said, "That's it."

Not hesitating, Sam Kyler stepped up to the thin panel, placed his ear against it and listened briefly. Then, with the shotgun in his right hand, fully cocked he pushed the door open with his left.

Rufe Eggert and a half dozen riders were grouped around a small table. Stacks of currency were before each man. Draped across the back of a nearby chair were Sam's saddlebags.

At the abrupt appearance of Kyler, closely followed by Wasco and Tolliver, the men leaped to their feet. The pock-marked outlaw Kyler had encountered at Marcia Ashwick's cafe, yelled a curse and grabbed for his pistol. Kyler's shotgun roared, filling the small room with deafening sound and a cloud of smoke.

Through it Rufe Eggert's voice yelled: "Don't shoot! For God's sake—don't shoot!"

Wasco and Tolliver strode past the crouched figure of Sam Kyler. Together they disarmed the men, stepping over the body of the scarred outlaw, and herded them into a corner. There were shouts in the alley behind the building as men, attracted by the shotgun's blast, gathered hurriedly.

Dave Simon, trailed by Thompson and Pritchard, came through the doorway. Thompson stared at the outlaws—at Eggert—at the piles of currency.

"What the devil's goin' on—"

"There's our money," Tolliver said. "Was Eggert. Had this bunch ambush Kyler and

158

Wasco . . . Expect it was him the other time, too."

The saloonman twisted around, shook his head in a vehement denial. "Wasn't me . . . Maybe this time—"

"Makes no difference," Shinn Thompson said. "Once is enough to hang you—"

"Hang?" Eggert repeated. "For just robbin'—"

"Never you mind," Tolliver said. "You'll get what you've got comin'." He began to collect the currency, paused, looked at Kyler.

"Reckon that winds things up for you two," he said. "We'll take care of these jaspers. Why don't you go over to the hotel, get yourselves some rest? I'll send Doc Patton over to patch you up . . . And Marcy can bring you a bite to eat."

Dave Simon nodded. "Looks like you can use it. We'll settle up with you tonight. Exceptin' for that I reckon you're all through here—"

"Not yet," a voice said from the doorway.

Kyler turned slowly. He didn't have to wonder at the identity of the speaker. It was Gates—the Dalhart marshal.

159

21

A HUSH dropped over the room. Shinn Thompson wheeled, his cane rapping against the bare floor. Coils of smoke still hung in the air and he thrust his head forward, peered through the rectangle of daylight.

"Who the hell are you?" he demanded.

"Name's Gates. Dalhart Town Marshal."

"Mite out of your territory, ain't you? What're you wantin' around here?"

"Kyler . . . I'm taking him back with me."

"You take him—you'll have to take the whole town—"

"Forget it," Kyler broke in. "No point in you mixing up in this."

"Seems we already are," Tolliver said. "Got somethin' to do with the drive—them outlaws, ain't it?"

"That's part of it," Gates said. "Got a wanted dodger on him, too. Robbery."

"So you come traipsin' clear over here after him, eh?" Thompson said sarcastically. "How's

160

it happen you never done nothin' like that before? Been plenty of outlaws come runnin' into this country but you high-powered badge toters paid them no mind. Was out of your jurisdiction, you told us. Was No-Man's-Land . . ."

"Little different this time, mister . . . Kyler done some killin'."

"Outlaws," Tolliver said. "You ought to be thankin' him for it . . . Saved you the trouble."

Sam Kyler listened. When it was again quiet, he said, "You're wasting your time, Gates. I'm not going back."

"I can take you—"

"You mean you can try. . . . If I'd done anything wrong, I'd be willing to go along. But I haven't. That robbery thing's a mistake. I got held up, but I returned the money. Few days more you'll be getting word the charges have been dropped."

Gates's expression did not change. It was evident he believed none of it.

Dave Simon said, "We know this much, Marshal. He got the money back, all right. Here in town. Most of us saw him do it. And he figured to send it back."

"You willing to swear he did?"

"If he says he did, I'll swear he's telling the truth."

"No need," Kyler broke in wearily. "All you've got to do is check with the teller in the Cattleman's Trust. He mailed the draft for me."

Shinn Thompson laughed. "Reckon that settles it, Mister Marshal."

"Part of it—maybe . . . Still the matter of those killin's . . ."

"Them outlaws? What's ailin' you, Gates! You ought to be pleased he done it."

"Still men . . . And it happened in my town."

"So that makes it important. Well—that's a hell of a way to look at it. It was fine for them to go on stealin' us blind—and you couldn't do nothin' about it. Nobody could. Outside the law, we was told. Then when we hire us a man to get rid of them, you want to jail him for it. . . . What kind of fool figurin' is that?"

"It's law and order—"

"Law and order! You sure got the wrong idea of what that means! Kyler's showed you what real law and order is. He broke up the worst gang in this part of the country—by hisself! He ought to be wearin' that badge, not you!"

"Reckon you could say he is a lawman—sort

of," Tom Tolliver said. "Maybe we didn't do no swearin' in or hang a badge on him, but we could've, if we'd a thought. Amounts to the same."

Gates bristled. "You've got no authority to appoint a lawman. This territory is un-organized—"

"But we're livin' in it and we're runnin' it," Shinn Thompson said. "All the authority we need." He turned to Kyler. "How about it—you want to keep that there badge we forgot to pin on you? Goes for your deputy, too."

Sam grinned, glanced at Wasco. The old puncher bobbed his head. Kyler looked at Thompson.

"Be proud to," he said.

Thompson nodded to Gates. "Reckon that settles it, Mister Dalhart Marshal . . . Accordin' to your own thinkin' a lawman's got a right to go after outlaws that're raisin' hell in his territory . . . Seems that's just what ours was doin'."

"It's not legal—"

"Far as we're concerned, it is—and if'n you don't like it, best thing you can do is write the President of the United States and bellyache to him about it. Expect he'll tell you we're within our rights."

Gates shrugged resignedly. "Let it pass," he said. After a moment he looked up. A smile crossed his stern features as he extended his hand to Kyler.

"Glad to meet you, Marshal. Want to wish you a lot of luck."

Sam smiled, took the lawman's fingers into his own. "No hard feelings?"

Gates shook his head. "Nope . . . Just one thing. Next time you've got a problem in my town, be obliged if you'll come to me first."

"I'll do that," Kyler replied.

THE END

BRETT RANDALL, GAMBLER
by E. B. Mann
Larry Day had the choice of running away from the law or of assuming a dead man's place. No matter what he decided he was bound to end up dead.

THE GUNSHARP
by William R. Cox
The Eggerleys weren't very smart. They trained their sights on Will Carney and Arizona's biggest blood bath began.

THE DEPUTY OF SAN RIANO
by Lawrence A. Keating and
Al. P. Nelson
When a man fell dead from his horse, Ed Grant was spotted riding away from the scene. The deputy sheriff rode out after him and came up against everything from gunfire to dynamite.

SUNDANCE: IRON MEN
by Peter McCurtin
Sundance, assigned to save the railroad from a murder spree, soon came to realise that he'd have to fight fire with fire, bullets with bullets and death with death!

FARGO: MASSACRE RIVER
by John Benteen

Fargo spurred his horse to the edge of the road. The ambushers up ahead had now blocked the road. Fargo's convoy was a jumble, a perfect target for the insurgents' weapons!

SUNDANCE:
DEATH IN THE LAVA
by John Benteen

The land echoed with the thundering hoofs of Modoc ponies. In minutes they swooped down and captured the wagon train and its cargo of gold. But now the halfbreed they called Sundance was going after it, and he swore nothing would stand in his way.

GUNS OF FURY
by Ernest Haycox

Dane Starr, alias Dan Smith, wanted to close the door on his past and hang up his guns, but people wouldn't let him. Good men wanted him to settle their scores for them. Bad men thought they were faster and itched to prove it. Starr had to keep killing just to stay alive.

FARGO: PANAMA GOLD
by John Benteen

Cleve Buckner was recruiting an army of killers, gunmen and deserters from all over Central America. With foreign money behind him, Buckner was going to destroy the Panama Canal before it could be completed. Fargo's job was to stop Buckner—and to eliminate him once and for all!

FARGO: THE SHARPSHOOTERS
by John Benteen

The Canfield clan, thirty strong, were raising hell in Texas. One of them had shot a Texas Ranger, and the Rangers had to bring in the killer. Fargo was tough enough to hold his own against the whole clan.

SUNDANCE: OVERKILL
by John Benteen

Sundance's reputation as a fighting man had spread. There was no job too tough for the halfbreed to handle. So when a wealthy banker's daughter was kidnapped by the Cheyenne, he offered Sundance $10,000 to rescue the girl.

HELL RIDERS
by Steve Mensing

Wade Walker's kid brother, Duane, was locked up in the Silver City jail facing a rope at dawn. Wade was a ruthless outlaw, but he was smart, and he had vowed to have his brother out of jail before morning!

DESERT OF THE DAMNED
by Nelson Nye

The law was after him for the murder of a marshal—a murder he didn't commit. Breen was after him for revenge—and Breen wouldn't stop at anything . . . blackmail, a frameup . . . or murder.

DAY OF THE COMANCHEROS
by Steven C. Lawrence

Their very name struck terror into men's hearts—the Comancheros, a savage army of cutthroats who swept across Texas, leaving behind a bloodstained trail of robbery and murder.

SUNDANCE: SILENT ENEMY
by John Benteen

Both the Indians and the U.S. Cavalry were being victimized. A lone crazed Cheyenne was on a personal war path against both sides. They needed to pit one man against one crazed Indian. That man was Sundance.

LASSITER
by Jack Slade

Lassiter wasn't the kind of man to listen to reason. Cross him once and he'd hold a grudge for years to come—if he let you live that long. But he was no crueler than the men he had killed, and he had never killed a man who didn't need killing.

LAST STAGE TO GOMORRAH
by Barry Cord

Jeff Carter, tough ex-riverboat gambler, now had himself a horse ranch that kept him free from gunfights and card games. Until Sturvesant of Wells Fargo showed up. Jeff owed him a favour and Sturvesant wanted it paid up. All he had to do was to go to Gomorrah and recover a quarter of a million dollars stolen from a stagecoach!